THE FORSYTHE STAGE

Town Marshal Sam Brennan had several mysteries on his hands. One was the condition of the Forsythe stage when it was found abandoned. Another was the pair of strangers named Douglas who arrived in town. Later, when it was least expected, Sam got shot, and when that was ultimately resolved by his friend — the local harness maker — Sam was flat out on the jailhouse floor unable to move.

C.1

CLIFF KETCHUM

THE FORSYTHE STAGE

Complete and Unabridged

LINFORD
Leicester

First published in Great Britain in 1991 by
Robert Hale Limited
London

First Linford Edition
published January 1995
by arrangement with
Robert Hale Limited
London

British Library CIP Data

Ketchum, Cliff
   The Forsythe stage.—Large print ed.—
Linford western library
I. Title II. Series
813.54 [F]

ISBN 0–7089–7685–9

Published by
F. A. Thorpe (Publishing) Ltd.
Anstey, Leicestershire

Set by Words & Graphics Ltd.
Anstey, Leicestershire
Printed and bound in Great Britain by
T. J. Press (Padstow) Ltd., Padstow, Cornwall

This book is printed on acid-free paper

1

The Abandoned Coach

IT was getting along toward the end of the rainy season, the ground was still damp, soggy in places, the grass was 'coming on', and human activity, which had been more or less restricted because of winter for something like six or seven months, had begun to evince the expanding activity which invariably accompanied new warmth, days without leaden skies overhead, and the release of cabin-bound or town-bound energy.

At the town of Forsythe in southern Colorado fresh activity included stockmen working cattle early, before it was hot enough for bot flies and screw-worms to infect the branding, 'altering' and wattling, occasionally de-horning, which left inviting wounds

1

for parasites, in the far ranges, and which encouraged freighters to take to the roads again, and to set all the operations to work which supported or in other ways served a town and its surrounding countryside.

Even the old codgers who lived in shacks at the lower end of town came out of hibernation, along with the traders, storekeepers and itinerant peddlers whose boxy wagons rarely traveled far when roads were quagmires or winter rutted.

It was a pleasant time for people with occupations which withered during winter, as well as a busy time for those whose livelihood depended upon using the roads and the trails, including stagers whose business flourished after spring arrived, moving people, light freight, occasionally bullion coaches with hired outriders.

It was also a time of increasing activity for people around Forsythe whose occupations, like that of Town Marshal Sam Brennan, had little to do with furthering business but without whose services Forsythe could have slipped into the kind of chaos other frontier communities had, or once had had, before the functions of law and order, mostly law, were monitored by men who were professionals at their trade, the way Marshal Sam Brennan was.

He was a deceptively mild man of no more than average height but with muscle packed under a taut hide. He had punched, pistol-whipped and shot lawfulness into the Forsythe area.

As Oliver McCann who operated The Forsythe Pleasure Palace, the saloon in the centre of town which had once been a trading post back in the days of Indian wars and buffalo hunting, had said about Sam Brennan, he did not look dangerous but he was if some ignorant or cranky individual tried to hooraw the town in which case the bull necked affable town marshal became a ham fisted enforcer of order who was as fast and accurate with a gun as anyone else who made his living behind a badge.

The local harness and saddle maker, Jonas Harwell, was a taciturn, lanky, tousle-headed transplanted Arkansan, a close friend of Sam Brennan who had upon occasion backed the town marshal when troublesome rangemen or freighters came to town.

Sam and Jonas were a hard pair to beat, and most of what they did was done in silence. Neither of them was particularly talkative, and while the harness maker's ordinarily grave demeaner was probably attributable to the fact that his wife of fifteen years died unexpectedly four years earlier, they still made a good pair.

Springtime seemed not to have quite the same sense of relief and subdued exhilaration for Jonas Harwell it had for other folks. Except for his weekly poker session with the marshal and one or two others, Jonas kept to himself, worked hard, produced fine harness and beautiful saddles, kept the coffee

4

pot on his stove for visitors but was not a very good conversationalist.

Sam and Jonas were having one of their visits at the harness works, coffee in hand with long silences between sentences, when the southbound stage came straggling in, late as usual, passed the window of the harness shop and caught the attention of the coffee drinkers because one horse was lame, the near-side coach door had been broken and tied closed with someone's red bandana, and the driver on the box handled his lines more like a farmer than a stager.

The marshal put his cup atop the counter and left the shop heading north toward the big palisaded corralyard. As he rounded the nearest old sagging log gate several men including Ace Billings, the yard boss from the Forsythe Stage and Freight Company, was standing with the rumpled looking young man who had climbed down from the box.

As the marshal approached the corralyard boss turned. "This here is

5

the son of that homesteader near the foothills. His name is Olaf something-or-other."

Sam was looking at the hitch and the coach when he said, "What happened?"

"All the kid knows is that when he went down near the road, the coach was standin' there, horses picking grass, one hurt, and not a blessed soul around." The yard boss turned. "Olaf? You know Marshal Brennan?"

The tall, rawboned youth turned and made a small smile. "Howdy, Marshal. Bjornson. Olaf Bjornson. I've seen you before."

Sam nodded. He knew where the Bjornson stump-ranch was but had never had an occasion to stop by. He knew Olaf's parents by sight, large, heavy people, hard workers who were pretty much left alone by local rangemen because the land they had homesteaded was mostly timbered and northward far enough through the foothills not to have been used much by stockmen.

Sam asked Ace Billings where his driver was and got a baffled shrug. "He wasn't on the stage. It was empty when the lad found it. But look at that door; somethin' happened, Marshal. And that lame horse. He was sound as new money when Rupert — you know Dan Rupert who drives for us — when Dan took the hitch and coach out day before yesterday for the run over to Edmonton an' back."

"Was it a money coach?" the marshal asked and got a vehement head-wag from Billings. "No. There could have been light freight in the boot, I don't know what Dan could have picked up at the other end, but as far as I know there wasn't no reason for him to abandon the stage, an' look at that door, it's been sprung to hell. Olaf had to tie it closed with his bandana."

Marshal Brennan walked completely around the stage, watched the yardman take the horses off the pole and paid particular attention to the near side leader; he had a noticeable limp. It was not a pulled tendon nor a stone bruise, the animal was favouring his left shoulder.

Sam took the gangling youth out front and asked for the details. All the youth could tell him was that he'd found the empty stage with a lame horse and a broken door. His opinion was that the horses had been run hard; they'd looked tucked up and dog-tired when he'd found them. His guess was that the coach had come a fair distance at high speed, like maybe the driver hadn't been up there or, if he had, had been unable to stop them.

"See anyone?" the lawman asked.

"No sir. Just the stage beside the road with the horses pickin' grass. Not another soul in sight."

"Did you tell your paw?"

"No. I was more'n a mile from home. I just caught up the lines, lined 'em out an drove to town, favouring as much as I could because of that hurt leader."

"How are you going to get home?"

8

"Maybe catch a ride."

Marshal Brennan led the way to his corral and shed out behind the jailhouse, rigged out one of the horses there and told Olaf Bjornson to lead his horse behind the farm wagon the next time his folks came to town.

He watched the lanky youth ride north out of town before returning to the corralyard. Ace Billings was not an especially worrisome individual. He was in his office when Sam walked in from out front. Ace motioned toward the pot atop the stove but the marshal sat down without a cup of coffee and asked about Dan Rupert, whom he only knew casually.

Ace cocked back his chair before replying. "You know Dan. He's a rugged individual, been a stager most of his grown life, good man with coaches and hitches."

"Drink, does he?"

"No more'n you and I do." Billings rocked forward to plant both arms on the desk. "Sam, it don't make sense.

Dan drove for me something like six, seven years. Aside from rock slides or snow banks he's come as close to holding to a schedule as anyone who's ever drove for me. Something happened out there somewhere. Dan would have stayed with his coach if he'd been able to. I'm sure of that."

"Passengers, Ace?"

"I got no idea. Maybe he picked up some over at Edmonton. If we had a telegraph we could send a wire over there. They got a telegraph. Had one for two years now. Sam, I can't even begin to imagine what happened, but I'll tell you this, it had to be somethin' pretty bad for Dan not to be with his coach. Could the kid help any"

The marshal was arising as he replied. "I don't think he told me any more'n he told you. He's a straightforward lad. I'll see you when I get back."

"You goin' to back-track the coach?"

"Yeah. When's your next north-bound leave?"

"Not until in the morning. I'd like to

know what you find, Sam. I'm not real happy about sendin' another coach up there."

The town marshal stopped by Jonas Harwell's shop on his way toward the middle of town where the jailhouse stood.

Jonas was interested enough to put aside his skiving knife and lean on the counter rolling a smoke as the marshal spoke.

He lighted up when Sam finished speaking, considered the dead sulphur match in his fingers and said, "I know Dan pretty well. He worked the clock around, got two little kids down at Raton south of the line he pays to have taken care of. His wife run off some years back with a travelin' man." Jonas flipped the match in the direction of a brass cuspidor, missed by a foot and considered the marshal. "Was there money or bullion aboard?"

"Ace said there wasn't. But he didn't know what Dan might have picked up over at Edmonton. Maybe passengers, maybe some light freight. Maybe even someone's money box."

The marshal turned to leave. Jonas waited until he was at the door before saying. "You going up there?"

"Yeah. Seems the coach came a fair distance with the horses running free."

"Then Dan wasn't on it," the harness maker said. "If anyone could stop a runaway it'd be Dan Rupert. I'll be at the saloon when you get back."

It was still fairly early in the day when Sam Brennan left town riding on a loose rein. He did not expect to be gone more than perhaps a few hours, he thought he'd get back by supper time.

His bay horse was up in the bit. He hadn't been out of his corral for more than a week and, like just about every other warm blooded creature, springtime had him feeling a little snuffy.

The Forsythe stage company serviced an area of several hundred miles mostly towns and villages northeast and northwest. It had an occasional mud wagon travel southward but most often when there was light freight destined for one of the settlements down there. Mostly, the southward country was serviced by another stage and light freight outfit. The Great Southwestern Company.

Actually, the road northwesterly between Forsythe and Edmonton did not follow a direct route. It was necessary to travel two miles due north from Forsythe to intersect the foothill road running almost due west for fifteen miles to Hortonville, except where there were protruding spits of trees coming down from the uplands; those places caused the road to veer southward in order to go around them.

It was those protuberances where highwaymen had waylaid stages, freighters and horseback travelers over the years. They were ideal for that purpose because hidden outlaws could sit their horses among the trees watching the road in both directions without being seen, and it was the first of those ambushing sites Sam Brennan headed for after making the westerly turn onto the main stage road which was, in fact, a military road built by army engineering units during the Indian troubles. It was a good road, wide, mostly level, with excellent visibility except for those spits of trees.

By the time Marshal Brennan reached the first protuberance he had been in the saddle about two hours and the sun was beginning its descent, but there would be daylight this time of year for some time yet.

He hadn't had trouble back-tracking the Forsythe stage. There had been other traffic, mostly horseback but also with an occasional buggy track, but coach wheels were much wider, following them was no difficulty. The problem was trying to figure where the hitch had started running. Not at the first spit of trees, so he ambled along toward the next one and by the time he got there the sun was definitely turning rusty-red on its way toward the higher mountains northward, and that made shadows appear. They did not interfere with the broad tyre tracks, but when Sam finally found where the horses had picked up their gait, he had to dismount and lead his horse while he concentrated on reading sign which was growing fainter by the minute.

When he abandoned the trail and turned back toward Forsythe the sun was teetering atop some saw-teeth ridges behind him.

He was not going to get supper as early as he had thought, but that was of little consequence. If he had not accomplished much, he had his horse slogging along with all the crackers out of his system.

It was plumb dark with a puny sickle moon when he finished caring for his animal and went to the wash-rack on the rear porch of the jailhouse to clean up before crossing to the cafe, which was well lighted and had a fogged-up roadway window.

Jonas Harwell was at the counter and did not look up as the marshal eased down beside him, otherwise most diners had already eaten and the cafeman did not looked pleased to have the marshal show up when he was waiting for the harness maker to finish so he could close up for the day.

Jonas used his cuff to wipe away the residue of his meal as he turned and said, "Find anything?"

"Where the horses began their run, nothing else." Nothing more was said between them until the unhappy cafeman took Sam's order and departed, then Jonas asked another question. "Any sign of Dan Rupert?"

"It was gettin' along toward dusk. I'm going back up there in the morning."

Jonas pulled his coffee cup closer. "The story's all over town."

"Yeah, it would be, wouldn't it?"

"Couple cowboys at the saloon a while back. They said they saw a coach heading east. They didn't pay

16

much attention, but there was two men on the box. Ace was in here eatin' when I got here. I asked him if Dan had a gunguard with him. He give me a disgusted look and said hell no, there wasn't no reason; Dan wasn't carryin' anythin' but some light freight in the boot an' maybe a passenger or two he picked up over at Edmonton."

The cafeman put a platter in front of the town marshal and walked away. Sam eyed the steak and fried spuds without making a move to attack them just yet. "Dan wouldn't have a passenger on the box with him. Passengers ride inside."

The harness maker offered no argument. "That'd be my opinion too, except that we don't know, do we? An' we won't know until someone rides over to Edmonton and asks around."

The marshal spoke around a mouthful of food. "If they'd put in that telegraph line . . . "

Jonas arose to dump silver beside his platter as he said, "I was figuring on going over there the next few days to buy some hides. I could go tomorrow. It don't make any difference to me whether it's tomorrow or next week."

Sam put down his utensils and looked up. "That'd save a lot of saddlebacking, would't it? I'd be obliged, Jonas."

2

Trouble

SAM appeared at the corralyard the following morning. Ace Billings told him Jonas Harwell had gone north on the early stage, which did not surprise the town marshal. He asked if Ace had come onto anything else and the stage company boss led him to a small pole corral out back where a lame horse was favouring one leg while he lipped up the remaining stalks of his earlier feeding.

The horse ignored both men as Ace Billing pointed. "Got some swelling."

The marshal agreed. "He would have, standin' in this little corral."

Billings settled against the pole stringers gazing at the horse. "Yeah, he would have, but he's got a mark on his shoulder." Billings flagged with his hat until the horse turned and Brennan could see the bruise. "Looks like he got kicked, Ace."

Billings nodded. "He's a ridgling. I always keep him separate. Wouldn't keep him at all if he wasn't one of the best harness horses we got. My guess is that he tried to nip another horse the way ridglings do, and got kicked."

They ambled back across the yard to the office and this time Sam accepted the offer of coffee. One thing was certain; whoever had ridden too close to the ridgling didn't know there was a ridgling in the hitch, which could possibly mean that whoever had made that mistake did not know the Forsythe Stage Company had a ridgling.

Sam sat down near the stove. It was still chilly. He did not mention his idea that whoever had ridden too close to the biting horse was probably a stranger; he certainly was someone who did not know about the horses that were put on the company's coaches.

It wasn't much, In fact, except for the fact that it suggested someone on horseback had stopped the stage; maybe more than one rider, and that fitted with the place where the horses had run away with the stage — near the second ambushing site, the place he had visited before turning back toward town — Sam knew little more than he had known before.

He finished the coffee and arose to depart when Billings said, "I still don't like the idea of sending coaches up there."

Marshal Brennan replied from the doorway. "You sent the morning coach out."

"I didn't say I wouldn't send 'em out, I said I don't like the idea."

"If they were highwaymen, Ace, they're fifty miles away by now. No one in his right mind would stay around after stopping a stage."

Ace nodded without looking pleased. "Can you track them?"

"I suppose so. After Jonas gets back."

"They could be out of the country by then, Sam."

"The ground's soft, they'll leave tracks," Brennan said, and closed the door after himself on his way down to the jailhouse.

It had been a stage robbery for a fact, but what happened to Dan Rupert? Highwaymen did not take people with them after a hold up.

Unless Dan Rupert had been one of them.

He really did not know the whip very well, certainly not well enough to make this kind of judgement, but he knew someone who did. He went up to the saloon, which was nearly empty this time of day, and settled against the bar as Oliver McCann put aside a ragged newspaper and came down behind his bar looking puzzled. The marshal was not much of a drinking man at any time, but never early in the morning.

Sam wasted no time. "How well do you know Dan Rupert, Oliver?"

The saloon man leaned down on his counter. "Fairly well. He's been coming in here off his runs for five or six years. Why"

"You heard about the abandoned stage?"

"Yes. So has everyone else. You think Dan had something to do with whatever happened up there?"

"All I know is that there was no one with the coach when a homesteader's son found it an' brought it to town. Oliver, did you ever hear of highwaymen taking a driver along with them?"

McCann made a crooked small smile. "Not unless the driver was a female. No, I never did, but then I don't know a hell of a lot about highwaymen . . . Not Dan Rupert, Sam."

"Why not?"

"Well, for one thing he's drove a lot of bullion stages over the years. If a man was going to rob his own stage he'd pick one with a lot of money on it, wouldn't he?"

"Seems likely," conceded the town marshal. "It's not a possible robbery that troubles me, it's the missing driver."

"Did you scout around up there, Sam? Maybe they left him dead back in the trees somewhere."

That was possibility, and for a fact Sam had not scouted up the surrounding countryside last evening. "Would he put up a fight if someone tried to stop his stage, Oliver?"

"Hell, what kind of a question is that? Dan's a good man, dedicated to his work, saves his money and minds his business. How can anyone say what a feller will do under some circumstances? But it could be; from what I've figured out about Dan, he wouldn't back off real easy. Go look around up there, Marshal. I sure don't want to think he's up there with the buzzards pickin' on him, but I wouldn't say he might not be."

The marshal went down to the cafe, ate a good meal and returned to his jailhouse office. It would be a while before the harness maker got back. He used part of that time going through his stack of wanted dodgers looking for highwaymen who were known to take people off coaches after robberies. It was too far-fetched; he did not find even one who detained hostages except long enough to rob them, but he did run across an outlaw named Cox, Herbert Daniel Cox, whose trademark was freeing the horses and turning coaches over. Why, the dodger did not say; they never explained the kind of idiosyncrasies that set one renegade apart from other renegades.

Ace Billings came down in mid-afternoon, not to enquire about progress but to say he had just left a man and woman who had arrived on the south bound stage, from down near Raton over the line in New Mexico, who had a lot of questions about the Forsythe stage.

Ace was slightly self-conscious as he said, "Probably they heard about it somewhere, maybe just interested. But they sure seemed interested. Even wanted to see the coach."

"Did you show it to them?" Sam asked.

"Yeah. The town carpenter's fixing the door, otherwise I'd have it back on the road."

"How interested were they, Ace?"

Billings shrugged. "They looked at it, walked around it and looked some more, then thanked me and headed for the roominghouse."

Sam Brennan gazed at his visitor. "I'll look them up."

As the yard boss arose to depart he asked when Jonas would get back to town. When the lawman asked why, Billings said, "He's got two pair of harness at the shop. I need at least one of them."

Sam arose and smiled. "I'll tell him," he said and waited until the door closed before putting his hat on and heading for the roominghouse. He had to pass the stage company office as he walked north. Both were on the same — west — side of the road. Ace Billings was nursing a cup of black java and saw the marshal pass. He leaned to watch and speculated. Maybe running to the jailhouse after those strangers showed up hadn't been a waste of time after all.

The proprietor of the roominghouse, who referred to his establishment as a 'hotel', was a former rangeman who had frozen his feet and wore bedroom slippers now instead of boots. He was a little cranky which he may have had a right to be. Before he nailed down all the outside windows about half his itinerant overnight trade left before dawn through those windows.

His name was Clark Hinman, and when the marshal entered the dingy hallway Clark was leaning down over a big sofa plunging his hand down both sides and in back of the cushions. He straightened up looking sheepish. "Last night there was a band of half-drunk drovers layed over. They was celebratin' something in here, lasted darned near all night."

Sam smiled. "Find much?"

"Two bits is all so far. What can I do for you, Sam?"

"A man and woman, came into town from the south today."

"Oh them, Mr and Mrs Douglas. I give 'em the room next to yours."

"Are they in there now?"

"I don't think so. I heard her say they could likely hire a rig at the livery barn."

Sam returned to the roadway and walked southward in the direction of his jailhouse office. He was interested in Mr and Mrs Douglas, but if they had driven out of the town he would wait until they returned.

Just short of suppertime he went down to the livery barn to make enquiries, but the Douglases had not yet returned, and all the dayman could tell him was that the lady for a fact was a real looker. Sam acknowledged that the way he acknowledged most such remarks from pimply-faced youths and was heading back northward with shadows forming when he saw the evening coach from the north enter town with slack traces and no dust.

He did not go up there, he angled across the road and sat on the wall bench outside the cafe. It was not much of a wait, but first he watched Jonas rattle the jailhouse door before turning and seeing the lawman across the road.

Jonas was not only laconic, he rarely rushed into anything. He sat down, thumbed his hat back, hunched forward and without a word rolled and lighted a smoke. Then he said, "Dan Rupert picked up two passengers at Edmonton, and a portmanteau the yard man over there said he thought belonged to the passengers."

"What about them?"

"Two men, one sort of lanky and tall, the other one about your height and heft."

"Rangemen?"

"The yard man didn't think so. He said they could have been drummers except that they didn't have no display cases with 'em."

"How about Rupert?"

"Same as always, the yard man said. Friendly, relaxed, businesslike." Jonas looked at his friend, "If that portmanteau belonged to those fellers, I'd like to know what was in it."

Sam stood up. "I'll pay for supper," he said, and led the way inside where men fairly well filled the counter bench and the cafeman was scuttling like his seat was on fire.

There were a few questions directed toward the town marshal about the Forsythe stage, but as a rule the diners were discreet.

Sam's retort to the questioners brought a smile among the discreet individuals. He said, "You don't need information from me, you'll make up your own stories."

Jonas ate like a man who hadn't eaten in a while, which he hadn't. He had nothing to say even after he had finished and was lingering over coffee. But the town marshal did. He told Jonas about the man and woman from down south who had been interested in the Forsythe stage and had gone buggy riding. Jonas continued to toy with his coffee for a while before saying, "There was a woman saw them two fellers off over at Edmonton. The yard man said she was as pretty as a yellow bird. Yellow hair an' big blue eyes."

Sam recalled the livery barn hosteler's similar appraisal without attaching significance to it. He and Jonas returned to the roadway and settling dusk. They stood a while in silence before Jonas said 'good night' and went hiking in the direction of his leather works where he had a lean-to out back which served as his bedroom and loafing area.

Sam Brennan made his final round of the town, lingered longest at he livery barn, but those people had not returned, which bothered the liveryman who could imagine no reason for people to be buggy riding in the dark, at least no reason he chose to mention, and the town marshal sympathised with him. They would return he told the liveryman. Sam would bet a hatful of new money on that.

He was right. Mr and Mrs Douglas did return about a half hour after Sam had left the barn to complete his final round of town before heading for his room up at the roominghouse.

The following morning he got a shock. He hadn't even unlocked the jailhouse, was in fact eating his breakfast when Jonas came in, sat down, ordered, waited until his coffee arrived then said, "You ought to go look at that stage."

Sam waited but Jonas was sipping his coffee and chose not to elucidate until the cup was empty. "Someone darn near dismembered it."

"When?"

"Had to be last night. Accordin' to Ace he went back there just before closin' down for the night. Wanted to inspect the door after it was fixed. He told me this morning everythin' was perfectly normal last night." Jonas watched the cafeman fill his cup again before also saying. "Ace is madder'n that devil who couldn't catch the crippled saint. He'll be along directly."

But Billings did not arrive at the cafe until the marshal and harness maker had gone their separate ways, Jonas to his shop to try and catch up on work he'd neglected for the trip to Edmonton, and the town marshal up to the corralyard after the yard boss had crossed to the saloon before heading for the cafe and breakfast.

There were two yardmen idling around the stagecoach. One slunk guiltily back to work at the approach of the lawman, but his companion, a heavy-set, dark and scarred Mexican in his mid or late forties, showed startlingly white and even teeth as he greeted Sam Brennan. He gestured. "Look inside, someone cut the seat, the back of the seat, even tore out the door pockets." The Mexican asked a question and also answered it. "Who?" he said, and heaved his shoulders up and down in an eloquent shrug.

The hostler's description was correct. Sam leaned to look past the repaired door. Someone with a sharp knife had practically shredded the thick canvas covering of the seats and their upright back. The same knife had slashed both door pockets, flung them to the floor and had gouged into the packing behind the pockets.

As Sam leaned back the yardman said something in Spanish and immediately interpreted it. "Whatever he was looking for, amigo, he wanted it very badly, no?"

Sam smiled. "Yeah. The question is — did he get it?"

The Mexican shook his head. "No, I don't think so. Look in back, in the boot. I myself put that box in there yesterday after the carpenter was finished. It was light freight for down south. Come, I'll show you."

The yardman was right; someone had pried the box open and flung half its contents of dry goods into the boot. To Sam Brennan it appeared that the searcher was frantic by the time he finished inside the rig and had gone to work on the box of dry goods in the boot. The Mexican was probably right if whatever he was searching for was not in the box, then the frantic searcher had not found it.

Sam went over to the general store. The proprietor was not around but his clerk was. Sam wanted to know what had been in that box of dry goods the store had sent south.

The clerk got big-eyed as he listened to the lawman, and answered in a squeaky voice. "Dresses, some bolts goods, six packets of bone buttons and a box of shoe horns."

Sam smiled at the clerk. He hadn't lied, Sam had found each of those items. He left the clerk staring after him and hiked over to the jailhouse to linger briefly before walking northward in the direction of the roominghouse.

Maybe he was chasing a will-o-the-wisp, if so it would not be the first time, but for some reason which eluded him, he wanted to know more about Mr and Mrs Douglas.

The proprietor shook his head. "They left early this morning. Most likely left out on Ace's morning coach."

The marshal asked to see the room they had used. The roominghouse owner led the way and stood in the doorway as Sam made his short and cursory examination, came up with nothing and was out on the front porch before the delicate fragrance of a woman's perfume left him.

He went to the corralyard but the yard boss had not as yet returned from the cafe. Sam intercepted him in front of the abstract office and Billing's anger had not entirely atrophied as he said. "That son of a bitch; I'm short one coach an' figured to put that one back on a run this morning. If I could get my hands on him!"

"Don't you keep a nightman around the yard at night?" Brennan asked, and got a sour reply. "Not since last fall. Nothin' happened so I figured to save the money."

"One other question, Ace. Did that woman and man who came into town yesterday on the south bound, leave town this morning on a coach?"

The other man's eyes narrowed, colour returned to his face. "Them two. They ripped hell out of my stage?"

"Did they leave town on one of your coaches this morning."

"Yes, damn it; if I'd had any reason to suspect them — "

"Which coach and what was their destination?"

"The northbound for Edmonton."

3

Along toward Day's End

WHAT Oliver had said at his saloon bothered Sam Brennan, but he could not go up yonder and beat the brush in the area where the runaway had started, and also ride fifteen miles to Edmonton to find Mr and Mrs Douglas.

He met Jonas Harwell over at the saloon. They took a bottle and two glasses to an isolated table and got comfortable before Jonas said, "If those fellers on the coach had a portmanteau with 'em, an' it sure as hell wasn't on the coach, why then it seems to me they either ditched it or got a wagon or maybe a buggy somewhere since they couldn't carry the thing on a saddle horse."

The marshal had not thought of that

portmanteau lately, nor did he allow it to side-track him now as he said, "It's maybe up yonder somewhere around that second spit of trees where I think the coach lost its driver. Maybe he's up there too."

"An' those two fellers who was passengers?"

"Maybe."

Jonas sipped whiskey, looked around the room, shifted in his chair and said, "Where did those folks go — the woman an' man?"

"They left town this morning on the Edmonton coach."

Jonas re-filled his little glass but made no move to raise it. "They won't still be over there," he said, and leaned to re-fill the marshal's glass.

"Maybe, an' maybe not," replied the lawman. "But unless I'm leaning on a bad hunch, they know somethin' I'd like to know. I want to talk to 'em so I got to find 'em."

"An' you want me to go over there tomorrow?"

"No, but I'd take it kindly if you'd go up yonder to that second spit of trees and scout around."

Yeah. For the portmanteau."

"Or some bodies."

Jonas looked down into his little glass. "This damned mess is gettin' worse as time goes by. Someone is lookin' for something, an' the stage driver disappeared, an' now there's a strange pair of folks sidling in. Sam, I'll tell you what I think: Someone hid a bundle of money on the Forsythe stage an' someone else is lookin' for it."

Brennan nodded. "Where is Dan Rupert, Jonas? And what'd be the point in wrecking a stage? An' one other thing, that damned portmanteau. What's in it, where are they taking it, and just how the hell did they pack it along if all they had was saddle animals?"

Jonas made one of his rare smiles. "You left something out. Unless those married folks knew there was supposed to be something in the Forsythe stage, why did they rip hell out of it, and for that matter, why did they come to town?"

Sam yawned. "Wish to hell they'd put in that damned telegraph last year."

They left the saloon to pause a moment under a starbright sky. The moon had been filling out lately but it was still not full.

Jonas said, "All right, I'll go up there tomorrow."

Sam remembered something. "Ace is anxious about getting some harness he left with you."

The harness maker got philosophical. "Y'know, folks drop harness where they take it off, it gets stepped on, rained on, wore out, and they bring it to me because they got to have it the next day. Sam, I been thinkin' lately, there ought to be an easier way to serve the Lord than running a leather works."

"Or being a lawman," stated the town marshal. "If you find whatever it is, let me know. Goodnight."

For taciturn Jonas Harwell the ride north after breakfast was pleasant despite the post-dawn chill. He did not get out much as he would like. Having spent his earlier years doing range work, pot hunting and a little freighting, he had developed a strong natural attachment to the natural world, and a leather shop was downright confining.

When he turned west to ride along the foothills and heard a stage coming he faded back up into the trees until it had passed. That would be the eastbound with Marshal Brennan on it.

Jonas was not the best tracker in the country, but then he did not have to be to locate the spot where the Forsythe coach had begun its wild run. Other tracks, quite an assortment of them, obliterated most of the sign, but not all of it, and where the harness maker dismounted to lead his horse, no traffic had crossed the burm toward the trees.

There was something back a ways that stopped Jonas in his tracks; abundant sign that several horses had been tied back in here for a fairly long time. What kept him in the area for the better part of an hour were some marks that had not been made by either two-legged or four-legged creatures. They appeared to be drag marks.

He walked slowly to the site where the drag marks ended. It was the same place where those impatient horses had been tied, and that, he told himself, solved the mystery of the damned portmanteau.

It was northwest a ways where it had been carried and where an effort had been made to disguise it under tree limbs and underbrush. It was old, scarred and empty.

Jason examined it closely then hunkered down to build and light a smoke. The only distinctive thing about the little trunk was the faint, almost ethereal fragrance inside it.

Jason smoked and studied the thing

and decided that whatever else had been in it, at one time it had held female attire. Perhaps not too long ago, judging by that tantalising fragrance. As he killed the smoke to begin additional scouting, he was intrigued by the empty trunk, and why its contents had been taken away with the outlaws who had stopped Dan Rupert's coach. Maybe for money, maybe for jewelry, maybe the Good Lord knew what, but it had been thoroughly emptied and since nothing that could have come from it was anywhere around . . . Why in almighty hell would renegades stop a coach, take a damned trunk off it, drag the thing back among the trees, then take its contents, like some woman's clothing, away with them?

He went back where the horses had been tethered and stood quietly as a band of rangemen loped past probably heading for town and Oliver McCann's establishment of delight, although it was not Saturday. Or was it? He waited until they were well along then turned and began tracking shod-horse marks where they seemed to head toward the higher mountains, a very primitive, uninhabited place designed by nature to support and feed a variety of wild animals, and to also, probably unintentionally, provide a hundred perfect ambushing sites.

The farther Jonas went the stronger grew the sensation between his shoulder blades that if the outlaws who had plundered the Forsythe stage had decided to lie over for a spell, Jonas Harwell, obviously tracking them was going to present an almost irresistible target.

He left his horse hobbled in a little sawgrass clearing of about three acres and went ahead on foot with his saddlegun slung carelessly over one shoulder.

The tracks abruptly turned east. He followed them until he arrived at a place where men had established a dry camp, and here, more uncomfortable than ever, found several scraps of paper wadded up and clearly flung aside. All the papers were editions of the *Albuquerque Daily News*. They were dated about a month earlier. Jonas ignored them and scouted the entire area, found where the horsemen had continued eastward and turned back to the dry camp when it seemed the riders were not going to change course again. In fact, obviously, they had gone north only to be hidden from sight of the road.

He wasted an hour reading those mangled bits of newspaper. They seemed to have been used as some kind of wrapping or perhaps a buffer, for whatever had been in the portmanteau. There was little in the papers that would interest someone who neither lived in Albuquerque nor was familiar with local events.

He stuffed them in a pocket, returned to the horse and went back down to the road where he turned eastward in the direction of the southward intersection that led down to Forsythe.

46

It was mid-afternoon with heat and a faint haze miles southward toward some very distant upthrusts. He was hungry and puzzled. He'd found the damned trunk, empty, and track where riders had ridden eastward sheltered from detection by the road.

When he reached town and put up his animal, tied the apron back into place, went forward to get to work, he thought he could still smell that fragrance. It was distinctive; it did not smell of wisteria or honeysuckle, or the geraniums everyone seemed to plant then forget.

He could not describe the fragrance even to himself and except for being annoyed at finding so little, he unscrambled a pile of dirty harness, heaved one set on the work bench and stood, hands on hips, scowling. The leather was so dry it was curling. There were layers of dried manure on the leather. One tug was unraveling because the tough double stitching had rotted, and someone had sewn canvas around the chain tugs, a not uncommon practice to prevent chain rubbing horses' legs, except that this well-meaning soul had not used thread, he had used wire, and that pretty well defeated the purpose of covering chain tugs; wire was as much an abrasive as were the links of chain.

Repairing harness was no particular chore but cleaning it was. Jonas set bleakly to work. No matter how much work he put into bringing the leather back to health and sewing protectors around the tugs the way it should be done, within a month careless dereliction would have the same harness back in his shop.

It was a bad moment for anyone to approach the harness maker, but a particularly bad time for Ace Billings to walk in asking when Jonas was going to stop riding around because the weather was pleasant, and tend to his work.

Jonas, head bowed as he wire-brushed manure off leather, went right on working for a few moments before putting the brush aside, gazing dispassionately at the stage company head Indian and saying, "You got any idea how much work goes into making a good set of harness? How many nights a man works late and how little damned profit there is in selling harness like this? I didn't make this set but I can tell you the feller who did took pride in his work. He double-stitched every strain point, he didn't use no copper rivets because they corrode an' rot the surrounding leather. He was a real harness man, Ace."

"Well, all I remember is that I got that set of harness thrown in when I bought a coach four, five years ago. What I come by for — "

"I know what you come by for. Sam told me you wanted your harness. Well, you're goin' to get it."

"When? Jonas, I'm short a full set. We cobbled together a set from scraps an' whatnot hangin' on nails in the harness shack. I got old Wilkins the carpenter re-upholstering the coach with the busted door. I got to send it south tomorrow. I need that set of harness before morning."

Jonas walked over and leaned on the counter gazing at the second set of harness, which, if anything, was in even worse shape than the set on his work table. "By morning," he said quietly. "You know anything about the kind of perfume womenfolk use?"

Ace's eyebrows shot up. "Perfume? What in hell's that got to do . . . Are you goin' to have that harness ready by morning or not?"

Jonas turned to regard the red face of the stage company's man. "Even if I'd started on it yesterday I couldn't have it ready for you by tomorrow morning. When I was a kid startin' out fellers like you could brow-beat me into working all night . . . That's the prettiest perfume I ever smelled."

Billings looked to be on the verge of a stroke, but he did not say another word, he flung around and stamped out of the shop. Jonas looked after him: Let him cobble up another set of harness, if he could.

Jonas went back to the table to continue the work of cleaning the harness lying there.

The day was well along when Oliver McCann came over from the saloon. He'd heard about Harwell riding out about sunup, and because Oliver knew how the harness maker and the town marshal peed through the same knothole, he wanted to ask Jonas a couple of questions. The first one had to do with the missing Dan Rupert.

"He give me the impression he thinks Dan was involved on whatever happened up yonder. Did he give you that notion, Jonas?"

"No, but I can understand someone wondering. Darned wonder the town hasn't made a connection and got the gossip mill to turning."

"He's not in town, Jonas," the saloonman said. "Been down to the jailhouse twice an' it's locked tight."

51

"He went over to Edmonton."

McCann's gaze widened. "What for?"

"When he gets back you can ask him, Oliver."

"You'n him are up to something."

Jonas offered one of his rare smiles and went back to work as though the saloonman was not there, and after a few more moments, he wasn't. He hiked irritably back to his bar with nothing to tell the patrons who always assumed a barman knew the most about what was going on. A lot of them did, but today Oliver had precious little to pass along to his patrons.

Jonas finished cleaning the first set of chain-harness and had the second set on the work table when the town marshal walked in sucking his teeth. He saw what Jonas was doing and said, "I figured you'd be over at the cafe. I can see you wouldn't have a real big appetite."

The harness maker mentioned all that he had found up yonder and the town marshal looked relieved. He had brooded all the way back from Edmonton that Jonas would find a dead stage driver.

"The tracks went due east once they got up where they couldn't be seen from the road. I didn't tag them but for maybe a mile. They were still goin' east when I headed back for town."

Jonas placed all those crumpled newspapers on the counter for the lawman to sort through. He also said that while the portmanteau was plumb empty, it smelled faintly of some kind of perfume as nice a scent as man would ever find this side of heaven.

Sam looked up from the newspapers. "Real sort of soft and maybe kind of saintly?"

Jonas nodded.

"When you got a second or two go up to the hotel and ask old cranky to let you into that room the strangers used. Sniff around then meet me down at the jailhouse."

Jonas looked mildly annoyed. "Is it

53

some kind of secret what you found at Edmonton?"

"Tell you about it at the jailhouse, I got a stop to make first," the lawman said, and left the shop.

Jonas went back to cleaning harness, curious and about half convinced the marshal had found something.

He was pondering the possibilities when he had to take time out to light two lamps. He hadn't eaten lately and he was not hungry. Not because of what he'd been doing, as the marshal had intimated, but because his mind was full of things that were tantalising enough to inhibit a man's appetite.

Ace Billings came back, watched Jonas at work for a while before wondering aloud if he could work something out to borrow that new set of harness in the shop window, which had massive leather tugs, not chain.

Jonas shook his head. "See how you take care of your own harness? Neither of these sets had been oiled or cleaned since they was new."

"I'll give orders to treat it real good, Jonas."

The harness maker finished cleaning the harness and stood back considering what had to be done next. For starters there was a badly warped, cracked and stiff britching. After that were worn-through places near the collar pad housing where the hames had rubbed.

"Tell you what I'll do," the harness maker eventually said. "That new set in the window is worth the forty dollars I'm asking. In fact it's better harness than your used to, Ace, and I hate to see you get your hands on it, the way you take care of things. But you throw in these two sets of worn out harness you want fixed by morning, and pay me thirty-five dollars, an' you can have the new set."

Billings' neck swelled, his eyes got their widest and dark colour filled his cheek. "You gawddamned highbinder, Jonas. You unscrupulous, connivin; snake in the bushes."

Jonas interrupted. "On second

thought, Ace, I won't sell you that harness. It's just too good for the likes of you."

For the second time the same day the stage company boss stormed out of the office mad as a hornet.

After he departed Jonas blew down the mantles of both lamps, tossed his apron aside, reached for his hat and went out to lock up from the roadside before heading for the roominghouse.

When he strolled past the corralyard Ace was in the middle of the yard telling two of his yardmen, with gestures, how that scoundrel of a harness maker had tried to bankrupt him. His back was to the roadway. The men facing him could see Jonas stride past and one of them, a husky Mexican with pock scars, winked and nodded his head.

4

Dan Rupert

BY the time Jonas had cleaned up, had supper and crossed over to the jailhouse, the town marshal had spent some time with the old gnome who ran the abstract office, and was putting out a brown-paper cigarette feeling somewhat satisfied.

He greeted the harness maker with an offer of coffee, which Jonas declined and waved him to a chair, then leaned on his desk as he said, "Jonas, you aren't goin' to believe some of this."

Jonas nodded, got comfortable and waited.

"To start with, I found that feller and his wife over at Edmonton. They had a room at the hotel." Sam Brennan leaned back. "It was him snuck into the corralyard and ripped hell out of the coach."

"Did he find his money?" Jonas asked.

"It's not money. I'll go back a ways; the lady an' her husband inherited one of them big land grants down in New Mexico. They was living in Amarillo when her grandfather died an' left them that big ranch. They went over there to take over an' to record her deed from her grandpaw. There was no deed. They went to the county seat looking for it to having been copied into the country records, an' there was no copy."

Jonas said, "In other words, she don't own the ranch."

"In order to get title she's got to record both; the original document an' her grandfather's will assigning it to her. She's got the will but it's not enough."

"Why isn't it? Hell, if he left it to her — "

"Because the old coot never registered

his deed. There's no evidence that it ever existed an' the county authorities won't allow her to take title an' possession without the original or a registered copy of it."

Jonas held up a hand. "Wait a minute. Is this where that damned portmanteau comes in?"

Sam smiled. "Pretty close. The lady, by the way her name is Ambrosia Douglas, an' she's as pretty as — "

"Ambrosia, for chri'sake?"

"Well, that's how those old Spaniards named their kids. Anyway, when she was a little kid she come onto her grandfather workin' over a hidey-hole in his bedroom floor. She rememberd that after her an' her husband went over the old house board by board, and when they found the hidey-hole there was the original grant deed from the Spanish an' later its Messican counterpart."

"They didn't go right away and have it recorded?"

"Didn't get the chance. A feller named Pierce, Judd Pierce who was her grandfather's *mayordomo* on the ranch, took her an' her husband on a ride over the ranch while two riders went through everything, including the portmanteau those folks had packed for their return to Amarillo and — "

"And found the deeds."

"Yep."

The harness maker considered the toes of his boots for a moment before speaking again. "All right, like I told you, I found the trunk, empty except for those newspapers which I figure someone used to wrap glassware or something in, but that don't explain how that little trunk got over to Edmonton, or who the two fellers were who had the trunk. Hell, if this Pierce feller found the deeds . . . " Jonas did not finish.

The town marshal was about to speak when someone rattled the door, then opened it. Both seated men looked up. The man who stood in the doorway looked haggard and rumpled.

They knew him by sight. He was the

missing stage driver, Dan Rupert.

Jonas and Sam Brennan were too surprised to speak for a moment. Rupert crossed the room and sank down on a wall bench. It had been a while since he'd been near a razor, or for that matter, a cake of soap, but he was not without a sense of the dramatic. He leaned back, smiled and said. "I looked for Ace but he wasn't around. You suppose he'll pay me back for the money I had to give an In'ian deep in the mountains to have somethin' to ride back here on?"

No one knew anything about that. The marshal offered coffee, Dan Rupert had just filled up at the cafe with both coffee and food. He looked from one to the other. The harness maker said. "Start at the beginning, Dan," which was what the stager did after getting more comfortable on the bench.

"Left Forsythe like I been doin' almost every day since I hired on with Ace Billings. Nice day, clear sky, a little warm for so early in the springtime. Made the swing west up at the intersection like always and boosted the hitch over into a little lope."

"Any passengers?" the lawman asked.

"Nope, a couple boxes bound for Edmonton. Didn't have a worry in the world. Went past that first robbers' roost like it never existed an' was bearing' down on the second spit of trees when I saw some riders loping toward me from the direction of Edmonton."

Sam Brennan asked how many, the driver said there had been four riders then got back to his recitation.

"Hadn't been much traffic, just some folks in an old wagon before I saw those fellers coming. Rangemen, from the looks of them. As they went past I waved an' they waved back. I figured they was heading down to Forsythe to let off steam, went a hundred or so yards past that second spit of trees an' looked back.

"They was sittin' in the road watchin' me head toward Edmonton. By the time I got over there I'd just about forgot them.

"At the corralyard in Edmonton they had that little trunk, which was put in the boot, an' two passengers, couple average-lookin' fellers."

"Rangemen?" the marshal asked.

"Well, they was booted an' all but they didn't seem to me to be professional riders. Anyway, I was on my way back accordin' to schedule and was passin' close to that second spit of trees where I'd seen them fellers on the way west, and they came down out of the trees, carbines hooked over their arms blocking the road. I hauled back to a walk tryin' to decide if there was a way to lash up the hitch an go out an' around them when one of those lads inside the coach opened the door, leaned far out an' aimed a big old cocked dragoon pistol at me.

"I stopped. Those fellers on horseback was the same four fellers I'd passed the day before on my way over to Edmonton. I told you; they took the little trunk off, told me to stand clear, and couple 'em rode up alongside the hitch an' commenced beatin' them with rawhide quirts.

"The horses run like the wind, I could see the rig was going over an' yelled to them, but they just sat there an' watched. I don't know exactly what happened, there was too much dust an' commotion, but I saw the off-side door fly open as the coach stopped. That door kept it from goin' plumb over. The horses was pullin' for all they was worth, the coach righted itself and kept going.

"The feller who seemed to be the boss sent them two passengers I brought along up into the trees where there was horses for them."

Marshal Brennan interrupted. "That made six of them, Dan?"

"Yep. The pair I hauled from Edmonton and them other four that was waitin' to ambush the coach."

"How long were you with them?"

Like everyone, Rupert had a limit,

although up to now it had not seemed he had. He scowled at the lawman. "You want me to finish this my own way, Marshal, or have you got — "

"Your own way," growled the harness maker, and threw a darkly disapproving look at the lawman.

"I told you they packed that little trunk up into the timber. They ransacked it. It had women's clothing an' what not in it. They went over that stuff like their lives depended on findin' something. I don't think they found it. They cussed a lot and flung things around. Then they had an argument about what to do with me. Them two fellers I'd hauled from Edmonton were for leavin' my carcass in some deep ravine. Right there I got the impression that them two and the other fellers hadn't known each other well. Couple of them rangemen gave them strangers a dirty look. One of 'em told that pair of gunsels if they'd done their job right there wouldn't be no problem now. One of the gunsels flared up. He said if Pierce had done *his* damned job them papers would have been in the trunk.

"For a minute or two it looked to be there was goin' to be a battle. The feller who acted like the chief In'ian fished around inside his pocket an' held up a brown envelope. 'Right here,' he told the others.

"Someone asked if he meant the deeds an' he said yes, they'd been hid in the head-liner of the trunk, when they opened the trunk an' went to ransackin' it, he told them to cut open the head-liner when the top was open an' found the brown envelope, while the others was flingin' clothes every which way, he opened the envelope, saw what was in it, pocketed the envelope and got on his horse to wait for the frenzy to end."

They told Rupert who they thought that head man was, someone named Pierce, former foreman for some big cattle ranch down in New Mexico. Rupert nodded. "First name is Judd. After they sort of hid the trunk they put me on a horse and sent me deep into the damned mountains with a feller named Hurley. He didn't say much an' neither did anyone else. But they told Hurley to meet them southeast somewhere on the trail back to New Mexico."

Jonas asked how Rupert had got away from the outlaw and got an annoyed look for interrupting, but Rupert answered candidly.

"I watched him like a hawk. Thing was Hurley was a lot more experienced than I was, he never let me get more'n a yard or two ahead, an' rode with his sixgun in his lap. I tried talkin' to him. Might as well been talkin' to a stone.

"We covered a fair amount of territory. The deeper we went into the mountains the more sure I was the son of a bitch was goin' to blow my head off from in back. I was gettin' pretty damned desperate; he kept ridin' behind me with that gun in his lap, not sayin' a word an' not takin' his eyes off me.

"We come to a little grassy place with a creek runnin' through it. He told me to get down, which I did before he led his horse to the creek to fill up. He was watchin' me like a hawk.

"Told me to get down an' drink if I wanted to. I said he was goin' to have to shoot me lookin' straight at him . . . A buck In'ian neither one of us could see, called to Hurley to drop the gun in the grass an' when Hurley started to twist real slow lookin' for the In'ian, the bronco shot into the ground between his feet. Believe me, gents, that made a believer out of Mister Hurley. He flung down his gun, an' when the tomahawk told him to lie face down in the grass you'd have thought Hurley was a gopher."

"The In'ian come out?"

"Nope. I never did see him. He asked who we were an' when I told him he said for me to take Hurley's belt and lash his arms in back, then tie his ankles an' to take whichever horse I wanted and get the hell back down out those mountains an' never come back." Dan Rupert made a wry smile. "He told me to leave my clasp knife, my bandana and my money on the ground. Which I did."

"An' it took you all this time to get back?"

"No. I tried to find those sons of bitches who stopped my stage then tried to wreck it."

"How far did you trail them?" the marshal asked.

"A fair distance. They was bearing almost due east. Eventually they come down out of the timber and took the easterly coach road a mile or so east of the Forsythe turn off."

The harness maker stood up. "You wouldn't have no trouble recognising those fellers, would you?"

"None at all," the stage driver said, and also arose. "If you had in mind makin' up a posse, Mister Brennan . . . "

Sam smiled sympathetically as he

stood up. "I'll let you know. You better roust Ace out, he's been worrying."

After the stager departed the two tall men gazed at each other. Jonas eventually said, "When you get that screwed-up look on your face, if I had a lick of sense I'd hightail it home and lock the door."

Sam laughed. "You wouldn't want to be left behind, to clean up dirty old harness and what not."

"What are you pondering on, Sam?"

"Takin' a stage east on the foothill road until we find them."

"*If* we find them. They got a fair head start. And New Mexico is south, not east. They'll quit the road directly, an' there we'll be, riding a stagecoach."

The marshal pondered a moment then agreed with his friend; maybe they could find the tracks, or even possibly the highwayman themselves, but New Mexico was south, they'd head down in that direction, not easterly.

"With fresh horses," the marshal said, "we could head on an angle and with any luck come out ahead of them." The harness maker smiled cynically. "Yeah. In a week. It's a long ride from here to there."

Ace Billings walked in, scowled at the harness maker but smiled pleasantly at the town marshal. "Them folks is back. They went to get a room up at the hotel."

Both the other men stared. Sam said, "Mr and Mrs Douglas?"

"Yeah. If that's their real name. Come in about half hour ago on the southbound."

After Billings departed Sam said, "I knew they were coming. They told me as much over at Edmonton. Only I figured it wouldn't be for another day or two."

"Do they know about their trunk?"

"I doubt it. I didn't know until I got back."

The harness maker stood in thought for a moment before speaking again. "The more time we spend talkin' the farther south those outlaws will get, and once they're over the line into New Mexico your badge ain't worth a damn. Tell you what, Sam. I'll round up three, four fellers and head south to try an' intercept them."

The marshal had to think about that, but once more, he could not be in two places at the same time, so he agreed, handed the harness maker a badge from his desk drawer, dispensed with administering the oath and told him, whatever else happened, if he caught up with those highbinders, to find the brown envelope with the deeds in it and bring it back.

After Jonas left Sam headed for the roominghouse. The handsome woman and her husband had just returned from the cafe.

Sam told him what he knew about the trunk and its contents. They became more intensely interested as he spoke; when he was finished the man named Douglas, who was a large, well-proportioned individual, grey at the temples, with blue eyes and good

72

features, told Marshal Brennan that after being on the trail of those renegade rangemen for so long, he would like to ride with Jonas's posse.

His wife clasped both hands and looked distressed until the marshal said Mr Douglas would never be able to hire a horse in time, that the harness maker and his riders would be gone, which Sam did not believe, but neither did he believe Jonas needed a posse rider who wore elegant button shoes, matching coat and britches, one of those little curly-brimmed derby hats, and more likely than not hadn't sat a saddle for maybe twenty hours at a time, nor slept on the ground, nor missed several meals at a time, in his lifetime.

He asked them about the deeds the man named Pierce now had, and the handsome woman said that if Pierce could get down to their part of New Mexico in time, he could record the deeds in his own name, and if the Douglases tried to contest it, even if they won in court, land titles throughout the Southwest were unlikely to be resolved for years, by which time Pierce and his riders could sell off all the cattle, the horses, and anything else that could be moved.

Sam Brennan explained about the limits of his authority. As a matter of fact the authority of a town marshal did not extend beyond the limits of his township, but actually, because distances were so great and lawmen so few, it was common custom for town marshals, even constables to enforce the law wherever crimes were committed. But that did not include adjoining states; for example, the town marshal of Forsythe, Colorado, could corral criminals a hundred miles from his legal bailiwick , but he could do no such thing if he crossed a state line.

The Douglases, who had been trying desperately to overtake the men who would steal their inheritance, and finally were close enough to accomplish their purpose, were not very interested in

Sam Brennan's discourse on the fine points of jurisdiction.

But neither were they candid enough to tell Marshal Brennan what they thought of his negative statement; they were polite and cooperative until he departed, then made their own plans.

Sam had already spoken to the gnome of a man who ran the local abstract office, but he stopped by again after leaving the roominghouse because he had acquired a little more information since their first discussion.

The abstract official sat with fingertips pressed together until Sam had finished speaking, then said, "I don't know about New Messico, Sam. Up here they couldn't get away with something like that. But then we don't have none of those land grants. New Messico's law as I understand it, is a jumble of Spanish, Messican, and gringo law. I'd hazard a guess that if those fellers can get down there and record those deeds, with them lads as owners, it would be legal."

Sam returned to the roadway. Except for stopping the Forsythe stage and robbing it, Sam actually had little to make a case out of. But in Colorado that was enough.

If Jonas caught those highbinders before they got down to New Mexico . . . Sam went up to the saloon for a jolt of Taos lightning. He was not a drinking man, but right now he saw no harm in visiting the local waterhole.

5

A Very Long Day

OLIVER had seen the harness maker and four other men leave town about breakfast time. He hadn't got a good look at but two of them, Jonas Harwell and Dan Rupert. It was Oliver's opinion that Ace Billings would have a fit because Rupert went off chasing some will-o-the-wisp with Jonas.

When Sam Brennan asked what will-o-the-wisp Oliver was talking about the saloon proprietor said, "A cash box that was taken off that busted up stage."

Brennan was so surprised he forgot the drink in front of him. "A cash box? Where did you hear that, Oliver?"

"From the young feller who swamps down at the livery barn."

Sam snorted. "You believe what that

idiot made up out of the whole cloth."

"Well, I saw them leavin' town heading southeast."

Sam was too disgusted to pursue the subject. He returned to the roadway in time to see a top-buggy turning southward from in front of the bar. He could not make out who the driver was but he knew that trim little rig with the yellow wheels and red undercarriage. It had been the liveryman's pride and joy last year when he'd taken delivery of it.

Sam walked down there and had barely entered the broad runway when he caught the fading scent that had impressed him before, where the handsome Douglas woman had been.

He was still standing there with his nostrils slightly flared when the raffish old liveryman emerged from his harness room chewing a stalk of cured timothy hay. He had already worked his way past the first joint and was chewing toward the second joint. Timothy joints were sugary to the taste.

The liveryman came over, spat out his stalk and squinted after his elegant top buggy as he said, "Real class, marshal. Them two is real class. I wish there was more of it in Forsythe . . . Well, what can I do for you?"

"For openers — was that a couple named Douglas?"

"Sure was. Real class, marshal, even though the woman's maybe half or a third Mex."

"Spanish," said the marshal. "Where are they going?"

"Constitutional, the gent called it. A drive out an' around to get the kinks out of their joints."

"No particular destination?"

"Nope. At least they didn't mention one, and them bein' strangers an' all, they wouldn't have one. Just going' for a constitutional is all, Marshal. More folks ought to do that; settles the phlegm and softens the marrow. Folks had ought to stir up sluggish blood this time of year . . . You know, they're real class. The lady smells prettier'n a summer sunrise."

Sam Brennan went back up toward his jailhouse, swung down the north side, led one of his saddle animals to the tie-rack and went to work rigging it out. He usually talked to his horse. Not this time because the impression he had gotten from the Douglases was that they were going to lie over and rest, and leaving town in the early morning in a rig was not resting up in Sam Brennan's lexicon.

He had little trouble locating the rig with the yellow wheels even though it had a long half hour's head start on the south stage road. There was nothing down in that direction for about twenty-five miles, which intrigued Marshal Brennan, until the rig abruptly cut inland on a northeasterly course away from the road, and here he had to be particularly astute at following because although there was an abundance of stirrup-high grass there was very little other man-high cover. There were, however, dips and rises. Sam took full advantage of them.

He had no idea where he was going to end up until, the sun hovering nearly overhead, he could distantly make out the east-west Edmonton road and those spits of trees where the highwaymen had hidden themselves until the Forsythe stage arrived.

Sam halted in one swale to climb down to rest his horse and roll a smoke. If the Douglases were heading back to Edmonton, why had they gone to all this elaborate trouble to disguise the fact? It would have been much simpler and would have saved considerable time to just drive north from town to the intersection, turn left up there and drive directly to Edmonton.

When he finished his smoke he went up the far side of his swale looking for the top-buggy. It was a considerable distance ahead and would shortly reach the road. He stood watching. When the rig got to the road it stopped.

Sam rode out of his swale on a northwesterly course where, if the

Douglases saw him, they would probably assume he was a rangeman.

He held to his bypassing course until some intruding trees south of the roadway offered a screen for him to turn directly westerly and ride until he was among the trees where he again dismounted.

This time there was no sign of the yellow-wheeled buggy. He scanned the road in both directions. There was no traffic at all, certainly no sign of the little rig he had been following.

Jonas knew the country where the coach had been stopped, knew where the portmanteau had been searched then abandoned. But Jonas was somewhere on the southeast trail of those men who had the deeds.

The marshal hunkered down for a long while, his horse dozing in shade behind him.

He had an idea the Douglases were going over the same ground Jonas and the outlaws had gone over. What interested him was how the Douglases knew this was the place.

He was about to give up the vigil and head back when the light rig with the yellow wheels came down out of some timber up head with the battered portmanteau lashed behind the seat. It was heading west in the direction of the Forsythe turn off.

Sam got his horse but did not mount. He stood watching the buggy. Why in hell do all that roundabout driving to get up here, if all they had in mind was searching the robbery site until they found the little trunk?

How had they known it was up there — if they had known, which they might not have, although they certainly knew where the robbery had taken place, and they certainly had tried to leave an impression they had not had that site in mind when they had driven northward from town.

Sam mounted in disgust and turned back the way he had come. He did not expect to reach town before the Douglases did, nor did he, and when he halted out front of the livery barn the liveryman smiled as he said, "Them folks come back. Had a real pleasant constitutional they said."

Sam swung to the ground and trailed his reins as he walked mid-way the length of the runway to look at the top buggy whose shafts were on the ground. The liveryman came back too, and spoke absently. "Damned louts a man's got to hire these days for hostlers. I tol' him to care for the horse out back then come wheel the rig into the wagon shed. He's had enough time to do them things an' milk a damned cow to-boot."

Sam walked completely around the rig, then stood near the off side gazing at the little 'box' which protruded behind the seat. There was no portmanteau; there was no sign of the ropes which had held it in place.

He left the liveryman bawling for his dayman to quit dawdling and park the buggy.

As he was caring for his horse behind

the jailhouse he tried to make sense of what he had seen, and what he had been told.

Feeling disgusted he went over to the cafe. Ace Billings was over there wailing to high heaven about a harness maker who was never on the job, particularly when he was needed very badly.

None of the other diners were interested. Neither was Sam Brennan until the stage company *mayordomo* saw him and leaned to asked just where in hell Jonas Harwell was.

Sam was tempted to tell him the biggest lie he could think of. Instead he simply shrugged and went to work on the platter the cafeman had put in front of him.

Ace did not pursue the topic. When he left he threw a scorching glare in the marshal's direction.

Later, when the lawman went up to Oliver's place to settle his supper, he received a few guarded nods and that was all. Even Oliver McCann was noticeably distant.

Sam did not spend much time at the saloon. He went up to the roominghouse, took his bar of tan soap and his towel out to the wash-house and made himself presentable, then stopped by the room engaged by the Douglases.

Frank Douglas responded to the knocking and stood in the doorway pretty much blocking Brennan's view into the room.

Sam was affable. "Some fellers from town went after those fellers from down yonder. Left early this morning. Mister Douglas, the feller here in town who runs the abstract office told me if those fellers can get down to your county seat in New Mexico an' record those deeds, they can most likely get title to your ranch."

Douglas stepped aside for the marshal to enter. His handsome wife was standing at the far window looking toward the marshal when he entered. He pulled off his hat and gave her a little old-fashioned hint of a bow. She smiled back as her husband closed the door and stood with his back to it.

Sam dropped his little bombshell. "Where's the little trunk?"

They stared at him. He went to the only chair in the room and leaned on it looking from one of them to the other until the man spoke. "We left it in the shed behind the hotel."

Sam nodded about that. "Tell me something; if those rangemen stole the trunk from you, why would they ship it by coach up to Edmonton, an' how did you two know that's what they had done?"

"We found out from the stage company in the little town near the ranch that they had sent it to Edmonton. In fact, when we first arrived here we decided to lie over until we could get the lie of the land. Neither of us had ever been up here before."

"If you knew your trunk had been sent to Edmonton, why didn't you go over there?"

"Marshal, we're dealing with some tough and ruthless men. Whatever we did, we had to very careful or they'd find out we were looking for them."

Sam could believe that. Neither Douglas nor his handsome wife would be able to stand up to six renegade rangemen.

"Why did they send the trunk to Edmonton?"

Ambrosia Douglas answered. "We don't know. But while we were over there one of the yardmen at the stage company who rememberd unloading the trunk, then loading it again, said one of the rangemen, a man named Jess Hume, used to live in Edmonton and still had kin over there. That may have influenced Judd Pierce; he certainly had to send the portmanteau somewhere once he stole it from us, and he undoubtedly thought the deed would be in it, because neither my husband nor I arrived with anything but the little trunk, and sent it ahead to be freighted to our home in Amarillo."

Sam had another question. "When you went up there this morning why didn't you use the road heading north?"

Frank Douglas answered that. "Because we weren't sure where Pierce and his renegades are . . . Marshal, just how good are those riders you sent to intercept Pierce before he gets down to New Mexico?"

"Good enough, Mister Douglas. If Pierce can be corraled those lads will do it."

"How many are there?"

"Four."

"Marshal, there are six including Judd Pierce."

Sam knew this and shrugged. "Those are fair odds."

As he went to the door he said, "Mister Douglas, was there anything in that trunk besides clothing and those deeds?"

The elegantly dressed man reached into a trouser pocket and withdrew his hand with a thick roll of greenbacks in it.

Sam stared. It was a lot of money, he did not have to count it to know that. Douglas put the wad back into his pocket as he said, "That's the main reason we went out to find the trunk today."

Sam nodded, he could certainly believe that. "They didn't find it, Mister Douglas?"

"They probably never would have. They ripped the headliner, tore through the clothing . . . Marshal, if you've got a few minutes I'd like to show you something."

Sam said, "Just tell me."

"The trunk was built with a false bottom. About the only way it would be noticeable would be if someone had the sense to measure the inside bottom to top, then measure the outside from bottom to top. There would be a three inch discrepancy."

Sam left the room, went out onto the dilapidated veranda and breathed deeply of night air. He could not fault any of the answers they had given him, and for a blessed fact if he'd owned a trunk with a false bottom full of money, he'd have gone after it too; maybe even more quickly than they had.

He went down to the jailhouse, fired up a lamp and went over the doings of this day one at a time. Everything that had bothered him earlier had been satisfactorily explained by the man with the handsome wife whose fragrance made it difficult for a man to concentrate.

He doused the lamp eventually and went out front to stand in the night wondering about Jonas and his posse riders.

He did not share the anxiety the Douglases had evinced although he did not doubt for a moment those fleeing renegades would expect to be followed.

He was about to make his final round of the day when someone stepped up onto the plankwalk, south of him, speaking calmly but with a thick accent.

"Good evening, Marshal. It is Olaf Bjornson."

Sam turned, eyed the tall youth and asked if Olaf's father was also in town. He had never seen the lad without his parents.

"No, I came alone, Marshal. My parents could not leave. They have an injured man. They found him trying to crawl from where his horse threw him in some rocks. The horse they have found no sign of, but maybe in the morning. The man used his gun to make my parents carry him to the house. My mother thinks he is badly hurt inside someway. My father sits with him. They tried to feed him but all he wanted was watered whiskey. I was in the barn. I didn't know until I came into the kitchen and my mother grabbed me, took me outside and said for me to come for you. She is afraid of the man."

Sam eyed the tall youth. He had questions galore but asking them could be put off until he and the tall youth were a-horseback.

When they were riding toward the north end of the town Sam asked if Olaf was sure the injured man with the gun had not known his parents had a son. Olaf was positive about that; his mother had hustled him out to the back porch before he'd more than barely got inside.

Sam asked what the man looked like and got a rueful gaze from Olaf. "I did not see him. I did not know anything about him until my mother collared me in the kitchen and pushed me out back. All I know is what she told me, which is what I've told you; they found him hurt in some rocks where his horse bucked him off. He made them carry him to the house with his gun."

Sam rode at a loose lope. Evidently his interesting day was not over with quite yet.

The Bjornson homestead was several miles northeast of Forsythe in some foothill country. There was some cleared land but the upper, or north end of the place was pretty well timbered.

Sam tried to imagine who the injured man was. He came to only one conclusion, and it did not have to be correct, but a man who used a gun to force people to do what they would have done anyway, had to be someone who thought in terms of weapons.

An outlaw, or perhaps a fleeing fugitive in which case there would quite probably be some posse riders on his back trail.

They could make out lamplighted windows an hour before they were close enough for Marshal Brennan to dismount and hand his reins to young Bjornson with orders to take the horses far out and around so they would not be heard from the house, and care for them in the barn. After that, the gangling youth was to stay with the horses. Under no circumstances was he to approach the house.

Sam had no difficulty getting up to the house, nor in slipping down the south wall close to a lighted window where he stopped to listen. Someone was talking in there but the words were too muted by thick walls to be distinguishable.

He returned to the rear of the house, grasped the latch tightly, squeezed until he knew the little metal bar on the inside had been lifted from its slot, and lifted the door slightly as he eased it inward. It did not make a sound. But the floorboards did when Sam took his first tentative step forward. He froze in place. Evidently the flooring that had groaned under him had not made sufficient noise to be heard elsewhere in the house where a man's steady voice was droning.

He leaned far enough to get close to a wall where there was less chance that his weight would make the floorboards yield.

He heard someone coming and looked frantically for concealment. A door was partially open which led into the interior of the house. On the back of this door where someone had embedded three large dowels, layers of cold weather clothing had been hung one atop the other until a thick, scraggly collection of heavy garments had been fashioned into several large, thick, hanging bundles. It was better than being caught in the open but not very much better.

Sam ducked behind the door, behind the piles of hanging garments, and scarcely breathed as an individual with a solid, heavy tread entered the kitchen.

6

The Brown Envelope

HE knew her by sight; although they had met a number of times in town, usually on Saturdays, he did not know Olaf's mother to speak to.

As he stepped into sight from around the hanging bundles of clothing he held a finger to his lips.

The woman was big-boned, large and work-worn. When she saw him she neither moved nor showed much expression. She turned back to filling a tea kettle with hot water as though Sam was not ten feet away.

When she turned back holding the kettle she whispered, "He is hurt inside. My husband feeds him watered whiskey so he is rational for short periods. You can follow me but when I

97

enter the bedroom you had better wait outside."

Sam nodded and jerked his head for her to leave the kitchen. She only halted once, that was to lean close and ask about her son. Sam whispered back that Olaf was in the barn with the horses and had been told to stay there.

The large woman went ahead, entered the bedroom where Sam could hear the monotonous voice droning and recognised it as the sound of Olaf's father, a large, powerful man named Henry, which may not have been the name he had been given at a christening but it was the only name folks in the Forsythe country knew him by.

Sam stood against the wall listening. Henry Bjornson's wife said, "Raise him up a little. Goot, now hold him."

A moment later someone wetly coughed and said, "That's enough. Pour some whiskey in the cup."

Sam freed the tie-down over his holstered Colt and eased a little closer.

Someone sighed and there was silence. It lasted until Henry Bjornson spoke. "We can't move you. I don't know how bad off you are."

"I'll be a damned sight worse off if you don't move me. You got a barn out back. I saw it when I rode past."

Henry's response stopped Sam Brennan in his tracks. "You don't need the gun. Put it down. All right, but we'll have to use the blanket as a stretcher. Mister, are you sure — ?"

"Just get me out to the damned barn."

Sam listened, guessed the Bjornsons were on both sides of the bed preparing to lift the man, and stepped around into the doorway. Neither Henry nor the injured man looked up but Henry's wife did. She saw the marshal lift out his sixgun without haste and point it. She straightened up without a word and her husband looked annoyedly at her, saw her expression and stepped aside as he too faced the doorway.

The man in the bed was the last

to see the lawman. When he saw the aimed sixgun, the stance of the man in the doorway, he did not even blink.

Sam told the woman to pick up the stranger's gun and put it on a dresser behind her. She obeyed and Sam finally stepped into the room, sixgun hanging at his side as he approached the bed.

He had an odd feeling about the man on the bed as they exchanged stares. He asked the Bjornsons if they had gone through the stranger's pockets. They hadn't so Sam did, putting the articles he removed into a battered old sweat-stained hat beside the bed.

Aside from a bone-handled large clasp knife and some money, there was not very much to put into the hat. Sam took the chair Henry Bjornson had been sitting on, put up his sixgun and was about to ask the stranger's name when Henry's wife pointed. "Inside his shirt, Marshal."

When Sam leaned to unbutton his shirt the stranger raised a shaky hand to prevent this. He and the marshal looked at one another for a moment before Sam reached, raised the unsteady hand and forced it to the man's side. "Just lie still," he said. This time the stranger made no attempt to prevent the lawman's search but his gaze was bitter.

Sam knew what it was even before he had the brown envelope clear of the shirt. He sat back making no attempt to open the envelope. He and the injured man exchanged another long expressionless look, before Sam sighed and said, "How did you get it? The last I heard Judd Pierce had it."

The renegade rangeman's eyes widened. "You know about Judd?"

"Yeah. About him an' his friends an' a lot more. How did you get it?"

"Took it out of his saddlebags when he was restin' before strikin' out for home."

"Why? Why did you take it?"

"Mister, there's a lot more to this than you got any idea."

Sam smiled bleakly. "Maybe. You

figured to get down there with the deeds before Pierce or the other fellers could do it, get the deed recorded in your name, and come up a rich man. That's not too hard to figure. What's your name?"

"Jess Hume."

Brennan nodded. "I've heard about you."

There was a long interval of silence during which Henry Bjornson left the room and did not return. His wife was now holding the injured man's sixgun and standing beside the bed like some avenging valkyrie of old. She asked Sam what was in the brown envelope. All he told her was that the envelope contained deeds to some land down in New Mexico and Jess Hume had stolen them.

She was more interested in her son. As soon as they could all hear Olaf and his father in the kitchen, the woman handed Sam the gun and went in search of her family.

Jess Hume said, "I had a good head

start. I was comin' down out of the trees north of this place when my damned horse stirred up some denned rattlers in the rocks. I didn't have time to get set. He flung me among them rocks like a rag doll."

"How bad hurt are you?"

"I don't know, but if I can't set a horse by tomorrow they'll find me sure as hell."

"Where does it hurt?"

"It don't hurt except in the side an' back where I come down in them damned rocks."

Sam arose, leaned, pulled the man's shirt up, and lowered it without a word. Hume said, "Ain't no bleeding."

Sam nodded about that and stood beside the bed for a moment before speaking again. "Did you work on the ranch described in those deeds?"

"Yeah. We all did. Judd was the rangeboss."

"It was Judd's idea to steal the deeds?"

"Yes. Him an' the old man were

pretty close. He knew the old man hadn't never recorded those deeds. What he didn't know was where the old cuss kept them. We searched before the old man's granddaughter an' her husband showed up, found nothing. Then they come along and found the papers hid in the floor. They was goin' to leave, had their little trunk all packed an' all. Judd figured the deeds was in the trunk, so we stole it and sent it out of the county."

"Why up here?"

"I grew up over in Edmonton. Got kinfolk over there. Judd wanted to get it out of the country quick so we sent it up to Edmonton, then we come after it."

Sam sat eyeing the injured man whose eyes were bright but whose lips were turning blue. He had no idea of the extent of Jess Hume's injuries but the longer he sat with the man the more he instinctively felt Hume had serious internal injuries.

There was no physician nearer than

the town of Edgehill, sixty miles northeast. Whatever the extent of Hume's injuries, Sam doubted that he could survive that long a trip in a wagon.

Henry Bjornson came to the doorway with coffee for the marshal. He did not look at the man in the bed but Hume looked at him. "You snuck this lawman into the house after I warned you."

Bjornson handed Sam the coffee and finally faced the bed. "Listen to me. I don't care who you are or what you've done, but unless you can get to a good doctor . . . You're bleeding inside. Look. Marshal, prop him up." Sam moved to obey. He had already lifted Hume's shirt. He knew what the injured man was going to see. His lower body was swollen and terribly discoloured.

Jess Hume looked, closed his eyes and kept them closed until Sam had eased him back down, then he stared straight up at the town marshal. "It don't hurt. Maybe that's just bruising from the damned rocks."

No one disputed him. Henry returned to the kitchen where his wife and son were sitting at an old table. They watched him fill a cup with whiskey and go back the way he had come.

Sam held Hume up. This time when he swallowed the motions were sluggish. Sam and the homesteader exchanged a look across the bed.

What had been a hostage situation became something else; even if they hadn't disarmed the injured man he could not have cowed them much longer. Time was not on the side of the renegade rangeman.

Sam took the brown envelope to the only window, opened it and examined its contents. He could make little from the Spanish wording but he was satisfied that what he now had in his possession was what a lot of people had tried very hard to find and keep. He thoughtfully returned the papers to the envelope and continued to stand over there looking out.

Sure as hell by now Judd Pierce knew the deeds had been stolen from him, and that, in Sam Brennan's opinion, meant Pierce and his riders would be back-tracking to find the only man of the crew who was not among them. It would require little more than basic common sense to understand what Jess Hume had done, and why he had done it. The same rules applied regardless of who had the deeds. Once they were recorded with a conveyance of ownership of the ranch to the man in whose name the recording was made, Jess Hume would have been the new owner.

Sam turned and eyed the man in the bed. He had to be a fool not to believe Pierce and the others would not be after him, would kill him the first chance they got. Had greed blinded him, or was he really foolish enough to think he could escape vengeance? Or perhaps it was both, but in any case Sam Brennan had no illusions, and one thing was a dead certainty, they would find him.

Henry Bjornson stood looking down for a long time, then leaned to look closer. As he was straightening up he said, "Come take a look, Marshal."

Sam returned to the bedside. He had to watch closely to see the injured man's chest rise and fall. He looked at the nearly bloodless face the closed eyes, the loose lips and stepped back. "Jess," he said quietly. "Jess; you hear me?"

The eyelids flickered but did not open. Henry put a huge, work-roughened set of fingers alongside the neck of the injured man, waited, then also stepped back.

There was nothing to say.

Sam returned to the window. Jonas would be scouring the southern countryside and sure as hell Pierce and his riders were no longer down there.

Maybe Jonas would find tracks, find the place where they had stopped then turned back, and maybe he wouldn't, but one thing a man could bet his life on, was the longer Sam Brennan and the Bjornsons remained where they were, the less their chance was of being able to leave without being intercepted and perhaps killed.

Henry Bjornson sat down looking at Jess Hume. His lips moved but there was no sound.

Sam returned to the bedside, spoke, watched for the flickering eyelids and spoke again. Bjornson said, "He can't hear you, he is dead."

Sam stood a moment considering the blue lips and bloodless features. "You got horses for your wife, you an' the lad?"

"Yes. In the barn."

"Stay in the house until I look around. Maybe we can get away an' maybe we can't."

"What do they want?"

Sam shook the brown envelope then shoved it inside his shirt. "This thing, an' they'll kill to get it."

"You think they are out there?"

"I don't know, but the whole troop

of us aren't goin' to ride toward town until I'm sure."

"What about *him*?"

"He goes with the house, Mister Bjornson. Maybe they'll waste a little time tryin' to find the brown envelope."

The homesteader arose with a groan and wagged his head. He did not believe the renegades would search for the envelope, he thought they would come after the town marshal and the people with him.

In the kitchen Olaf and his mother were indifferently eating. When the marshal and Henry walked in they both looked up. Henry gently wagged his head. No one asked what that signified, they knew.

Sam stood a while looking out, searching as much of the area he could see from the window above the sink. If they were out there . . . The woman asked how far they had to come and Sam shrugged because he had no idea. When he went to the door the Bjornsons watched him. He smiled slightly, opened the door and stepped out onto the roofed-over back porch.

The land was empty, silent and dark with a trace of chill in the air. Sam thought it was close to daybreak and was surprised; he had no idea he'd been inside so long. He also did not like what this could mean; Pierce and his riders could almost certainly have got back this far by dawn, unless they had made a dry camp somewhere, which Sam doubted; in their boots he would not even have rested the horses, there was entirely too much at stake. Wealth enough for them all not to have to work for a very long time.

He left the house keeping as much as possible to shadows and dark places, got almost over to the barn when he picked up a quick, sharp sound coming from inside the barn. He paused to categorise it; it could have been made by a shod horse or it could have been made by something else, but one thing Sam was sure it was not, was creaking boards or other signs of cold seeping into old wood.

He changed course, got around to the front of the house, gauged the distance to a stand of fruit trees, the only worthwhile shelter after he left the house, and waited for some indication that whoever was in the barn might also be outside of it, found nothing and made the crossing into the little orchard as swiftly as he could without making a noise.

He made an understandable and unfortunate mistake. He was not the only one among trees. The difference was that the other man had watched Sam sidle along the side of the house, then start for the sheltering trees, and he was waiting.

Sam saw nothing and heard nothing until someone close by in the shadowy darkness cocked a handgun. It was a sound once heard, was never forgotten. Sam did not move. In fact he scarcely breathed as he waited.

It was a long wait. The invisible

man with the cocked sixgun was in no hurry. Sam was motionless waiting to hear movement so he could at least place the position of his adversary.

When the man spoke he sounded bleakly satisfied. "Well now, I never figured it'd be the law. Ease the gun out real careful an' let it drop."

Sam obeyed. He had placed the tree where the man was hiding.

"Now then, Mister Lawman, who-all's in the house."

"The homesteader, his wife and son."

"And Jess Hume?"

"Yes."

"We figured so. Saw his horse a mile or such a matter southwesterly. Backtracked it by the full moon. How'd it get away from him?"

"Bucked him off in some rocks close by. The homesteader an' his wife carried him into the house."

"Hurt bad, is he?"

"Bad enough," the marshal answered before asking a question. "That ought to please you, one less to share the loot

113

from that ranch with, eh?"

The man behind the trees seemed surprised. "You know a lot for a feller who ain't got no interest. Jess tell you about the ranch, did he? Judd'll kill him for that."

"Judd can save the bullet," Sam replied. "He's already dead."

This time the invisible gunman was really surprised. "Jess is dead?"

"That's what I just said."

"What happened? You shoot him?"

"His horse pitched him off in some rocks, busted him up inside. He died a few minutes back."

The gunman was quiet so long Sam was beginning to wonder if he was still over there, then he said, "Well now, Marshal, let's stroll over to the barn. Judd'll want to hear all this. An' Marshal, remember, you ain't got a gun an' I have."

The barn was eastward about six or eight hundred feet. There was a fenced-in large patch of garden vegetables northward. Sam paused once to look back. His captor said, "Don't worry, I'm still back here."

Sam paused where manured straw had been pitched from wooden windows in the side of the barn. His captor moved around to reach for the door. He grinned at Sam, then tugged and jerked until the door began to yield. Sam dropped something and stamped it into the loose manure before his captor had the door open. He kept Sam from entering by putting a hand on his shoulder as he leaned and called into the interior darkness. "Got me a surprise for you, gents."

Someone growled back. "That gawdamned sod buster?"

"No sir. I got a genuine officer of the law."

A pale light appeared from behind a blanket. They stared as Sam walked toward their resting place. One rangeman snickered. "You sure do. Hank. That there's the town marshal from down at Forsythe."

A lanky, rawboned man stood up.

Sam was sure he had never seen him before, but evidently the rawboned man had seen Sam because he said, "Well now, Marshal. I won't say this is a real pleasure seein' you again, but it's sure a break in the monotony of waitin' for sunrise before we bust into the homesteader's shack and drag — "

"He's dead," Sam's captor said.

They stared at him. So did the tall, rawboned man. "Who is dead?" he asked and got a quick answer, this time from Marshal Brennan. "Jess Hume. He got bucked off in some rocks, busted up his insides and he died in there about half hour ago."

The silence was almost tangible. The rawboned man remained facing Marshal Brennan. He eventually said, "How about those stump jumpers? They got guns?"

"If you mean are they goin' to fight you, I'd say no, they aren't. They found your friend and packed him to the house. That's the end of it for them."

A wiry, wizened older rider looked quizzically at Sam. "How come you to be out here?"

Sam looked the wizened man in the eye when he answered. "I loaned their boy a horse a few days back. Came out to get it."

"In the dark?"

"No better time if a man's busy all day."

The renegades hunkered down inside their blankets with nothing to say until the rawboned man eventually arrived at a decision and scowled at Sam as he said, "All right. Maybe you're lyin' but I can't imagine why. Anyway, we're all goin' over to the house with you out front. You tell them folks inside we want to see the body. You understand?"

Sam nodded woodenly hoping against hope that when the outlaws were inside looking around and asking questions, none of the Bjornsons would mention the brown envelope.

7

A Warning Finger

PIERCE and his crew were a rough, unwashed and unshorn gathering of hard-riders, the kind of men who took adversity to be a normal way of life. Pierce himself, aside from having the grainy, durable look common to men of his build and type, also impressed Sam Brennan as ruthless as well as shrewd.

Sam hunkered among them watching them eat jerky and dried apples. They paid him very little attention now that the novelty of his presence had worn off. Only one of them, younger than the others but equally as motivated, even spoke to Sam. He wanted to know more about the passing of Jess Hume, who had been a friend of his up until Jess had disappeared along with the brown envelope from Judd Pierce's saddlebag.

There was little Sam could add to what he had already told them, but since several men were now watching him he said, "He swelled up like a toad and turned sort of purple. He bled to death internally."

The younger man said, "From fallin' in the rocks?"

Sam shrugged. "I guess things like that happen. I don't know any more, except that it took him a while to die."

Pierce entered the conversation. "You searched him?"

"Emptied his pockets of the usual clutter a feller has on him."

Now they were all watching the marshal. "Nothin' else?" Pierce asked and got a head shake for an answer. Pierce became intent. "How about inside his boots, or maybe inside his britches?"

Sam gave a wooden-face reply. "Mister, you can see for yourself.

We didn't take his clothes off nor his boots."

They continued to regard Sam from wary faces until Pierce stood up. "It's light enough," he told them, and shook a warning finger in Brennan's direction. "Just walk ahead of us to the back porch. Don't knock, just walk in."

Sam arose among them, moved to the side door of the barn, the same door he had entered by, and from directly behind him the man with the raffish smile and faintly drawling accent who had captured him, softly said, "Mister, you got nothing' to worry about; just do like you're told."

Sam had no intention of doing anything else. As he led off in the direction of the house he had only one thought uppermost in his mind: Would one of the Bjornsons let anything slip about the brown envelope? If they did, Sam Brennan would have plenty to worry about.

When they reached the porch and Sam reached for the door latch, the men behind him fanned out a little.

The door was barred from the inside. Sam raised a fist to lightly knock as he called out, "It's me, Marshal Brennan."

Someone lifted away the door bar and started to swing the panel inward when Judd Pierce stepped ahead and gave the door a violent shove.

Olaf was swung against the wall. His mother was standing by the kitchen table and did not move as her kitchen filled with men she had never seen before behind the town marshal.

Olaf recovered and stepped from behind the door. That wizened older rangeman whose name was Ezra Bowman pointed a six gun without being very ferocious about it and jerked his head for the tall youth to go over by his mother.

Both the lad and his mother looked bitterly at Sam Brennan as Judd Pierce shouldered through and left the kitchen. Two men went with him.

Ezra Bowman wrinkled his nose.

"Anythin' to eat that's hot?" he asked. Olaf's mother, a head taller and half again as thick, looked down her nose as she said, "You need a bath!"

Someone snickered. It was not the wizened man. He looked coldly at the woman, raised his sixgun, cocked it and aimed it at her son. "Anythin' warm to eat?" he asked again.

The woman shouldered through to the stove and became grimly occupied over there. The men watched her and helped themselves from a large old speckle-ware coffee pot, but the wizened older man left the room to find Pierce.

When he found him he stopped in the doorway. Pierce and another couple of men had stripped the corpse. The contrast between white skin and enormously swollen parts of the same body shocked Ezra. Pierce looked toward the doorway as he kicked a pile of clothing on the floor. "Nothing. Not a damned thing."

Ezra seemed mesmerised at the sight

of the corpse when he said, "He had it, didn't he, Judd? You said it was gone from — "

"Of course the son of a bitch had it."

One of the other men at the bedside offered an opinion. "He cached it somewhere. Maybe in them rocks where he got jumped off."

"Maybe," Judd Pierce said, looking malevolently at the corpse, "In this damned house, or maybe these folks found it."

No one bothered throwing a blanket over the corpse as they trooped back to the kitchen where Henry was serving men at the table as fast as his wife handed him a platter of food. One of the men from the bedroom started to say something and Judd Pierce growled him into silence as he pulled a stool up to the table. Nothing was said as food was brought and the rangemen ate it. Occasionally one of the Bjornsons would spare a bitter look for Marshal Brennan. One of those bleak glares was intercepted by the drawling man who had captured the marshal, and he held his eating utensils upright in both hands as he addressed the large woman. "Lady, these here is the finest flapjacks I ever ate. Only thing they need is some blueberries cooked into them . . . And don't be mad at the marshal; he didn't have no choice once he blundered into us. If you want to be disgusted at him, ma'am, you got the right for a fact. He let hisself get captured like a schoolboy."

Judd Pierce looked at each of the Bjornsons individually as he ate. He said nothing. Neither did the others which left the raffish individual with the slight accent of Texas or somewhere down there, to respond when Henry Bjornson asked why they had come to his homestead.

"You got to understand," he told Henry Bjornson, "that fellers in our trade look after one another. Now that poor gent in there was one of us for quite a spell. When he turned up missing, Mister Squatter, we just naturally come back lookin' for him."

Henry Bjornson stood gazing at the smiling, raffish man. He may have had a sense of humour but there was no sign of it as he replied to the man with the faint accent.

"You come back looking for him, eh? An' you busted into my house with guns in your hands to find him? Anyone else would have knocked on the door but maybe where you come from people don't have manners."

Sam Brennan held his breath. He had judged the raffish man some time ago. He was one of those smiling, easy-moving men who would laugh as they took offense, and shoot.

It was a sound judgement and might have been proven so except that Judd Pierce had finished eating and stood up from the table, an action which ensured the attention of everyone in the room.

He looked from Henry Bjornson to his wife, then to his son as he said, "What did you folks do with the things you took off the dead man?"

All three Bjornsons looked blank. Henry finally jerked his head in Sam Brennan's direction. "He put things from his pockets into his hat. It was beside the bed."

Judd Pierce looked steadily at the big, thick farmer. "We saw what was in the hat. We're looking for something else you took off him."

Sam was watching Henry, whose face coloured as he looked steadily at Pierce. "We didn't take anything else off him. Just what I told you."

Sam was impressed by the home-steader's blunt and forceful statement. So, evidently, were several of the men at the table. Judd Pierce stared steadily at the homesteader over a moment of silence before speaking again.

"Did you catch his horse?"

Henry's reply was in the same forceful tone of voice. It was obvious to Sam, and probably to the others, that the homesteader did not like Judd Pierce.

"No. We never saw his horse."

The wizened man addressed Judd Pierce. "I told you we should have caught the damned thing when we seen it."

Pierce ignored this statement. His attention was fully on Henry Bjornson and for the first time Sam Brennan was beginning to breathe a little easier. Pierce looked from the man to his son. "What's your name, boy?"

"Olaf."

Pierce barely inclined his head. "Olaf. Well now, Olaf, tell me straight out — what else was taken off our dead friend?"

"What my father said. The things we put in his hat."

Ezra the wizened older rangeman was tiring of this. He went to the stove and re-filled his cup with coffee. From over there he spoke to Judd Pierce. "It was in his saddlebags as sure as we're settin' around here."

The garrulous man with the slight accent agreed. "We can find the horse, Judd, an' it'll be on our way southward."

Sam Brennan was reaching for his coffee cup when Judd Pierce smiled at Olaf as he said, "Naw; we all knew Jess. He had the makings of a fortune in his possession. If it had been in his saddlebags he'd have got these folks to go find his horse and bring it back here. Jess wouldn't just lie down an' die without doin' something. Ezra, you rode with Jess a lot."

The wizened man returned to the table with his coffee. Sam thought he was beginning to waver when he replied to Judd Pierce. "You figure he had the brown envelope on him, maybe in a pocket or in his boot?"

Pierce nodded. "What I'm figurin' is that he had it on him when these folks carried him in here to die."

"What the hell good would it be to them?" Ezra asked, and got an answer that it seemed to Sam Brennan had probably been in Pierce's mind before he had arisen from the table.

128

"Partner, it'd be worth an awful lot to anyone. Maybe they don't have any idea how much it would be worth, but it wouldn't take a heap of brains to figure out that if Jess was running with it, risked his damned life for it, it had to be worth a hell of a lot more than a field of pinto beans would be worth when they were harvested."

Sam could tell from the expressions on the faces of the men at the table that they were ready to listen to Judd Pierce, and he did not leave them waiting very long. When he resumed speaking he sounded to Marshal Brennan like a school master explaining something simple to a roomful of half-wits.

"They found the damned brown envelope and got it hid, most likely figurin' on keepin' it hid until they could figure out what was so valuable about it. Pierce grinned wolfishly at young Olaf. "They'll tell us where they hid it."

Henry Bjornson and his wife stood like oak trees looking at Judd Pierce.

Sam guessed they probably thought something bad was in the offing without having any idea what it could be.

But Sam Brennan could guess from the way Pierce had been watching the gangling youth. He put his coffee cup aside as Judd Pierce gestured toward the stove behind Henry's wife. "Hank, open the oven door." As the garrulous man arose to obey Judd Pierce smiled at the Bjornsons. "I'll explain how this works, folks. First we peel off the lad's boots an' socks, then we take a chair over there an' set him on it . . . Then we shove both his bare feet into the oven."

Sam saw the look of horror spread across the woman's face. Her husband's earlier defiance wilted even as Sam watched the rangemen yank the youth around so they could pull off his boots. They did not have to bother with socks, Olaf did not wear them.

A chair was taken over there. Henry Bjornson shot a look at Sam Brennan. Sam could not tell whether it was a pleading look or an angry look. Judd Pierce watched Olaf struggle as he was dragged to the chair in front of the hot oven. His father turned to Judd Pierce. "What kind of a man are you? Even the barbarians where I came from did not do such a thing."

Judd was unmoved as he watched two men struggling to hold Olaf on the chair.

Sam could feel colour leaving his face. He quietly addressed Pierce. If there had been any way to doubt that Pierce was bluffing, he would have kept silent, but the look in the rawboned man's face left no room for that.

"I got it," Sam said. "The lad don't know anythin' about it. Set him loose an' I'll give it to you."

Pierce turned slowly to regard the lawman. He had been in no hurry before and he was in no hurry now. "You'll give me what, lawman?"

"The brown envelope with the deeds in it."

The room was so quiet birdsong

from the direction of the barn was clearly audible.

Pierce did not hurry. "Jess had it — where?"

"Inside his shirt."

Pierce turned a beaming look upon Ezra. "I told you. He wouldn't leave it in his saddlebags. He wouldn't let it out of sight for ten seconds."

Sam reiterated what he'd said earlier. "Turn the lad loose."

Judd Pierce was agreeable. "Be glad to, lawman, the minute you hand me the brown envelope."

"It's not in the house."

"Where is it?"

"In the manure pile beside the door leadin' inside the barn on the west side."

Pierce looked at the garrulous man who had captured Brennan. "You'n couple others go look for it. Be quick about it, the sun's climbin' an' we wasted a lot of time around here."

Ezra murmured, "Amen," under his breath and raised the coffee cup.

While they waited Judd Pierce went to lean on the wall as he regarded Sam Brennan. "You're goin' to pay for holdin' us up, mister."

"You're gettin' the deeds aren't you?"

"We'd have got them anyway. These clod hoppers wouldn't have held out. Marshal, same thing's goin' to happen to you as happened to that stage driver. You're goin' for a little one-way ride."

Sam looked at the rawboned man from an expressionless face. That would-be assassin who was supposed to meet his friends southward somewhere, was not going to meet them; the stage driver had not been shot in the back.

There was no conversation as the people in the house waited for the men to return from the barn area. Olaf's mother helped him with his boots, which seemed to embarrass the boy. His father pulled a chair around and straddled it. He occasionally shot a look in Judd Pierce's direction and Sam guessed Bjornson's thoughts were not charitable.

One of the men at the table went restlessly to the back door to look out. He suddenly laughed as he pulled back inside. "Ma'am, if I was you," he said, "I wouldn't let neither of 'em back in the house."

No one responded to this crude bit of humour.

Eventually Judd Pierce crossed to the door and looked out. He raised his voice slightly as he said, "It took you long enough." The answer he got back was brusque. "You ever dig in a manure pile?"

"Did you find it?"

Someone outside approaching the porch said, "Is this it? If it ain't you'll have to get someone else to dig in there."

Pierce stepped out onto the porch as his two diggers came inside, and the rangeman who had been the first one to go to the door, curled his lip. "You fellers didn't smell real pretty before, but right now — "

"We got it!" Judd Pierce exclaimed from the rear doorway, and waved the brown envelope. He became brisk again. "Load your pockets with grub an' let's see how much ground we can put behind us before sundown."

Sam was left in the kitchen with the Bjornsons. After a while Henry said, "I figured what they wanted."

Sam nodded. "You did real well. All of you. Well, they got it so maybe they'll be on their way."

Henry gazed at the town marshal. "What about you? That big feller don't care much for you . . . I've got a sixgun."

Sam went to the door where he could hear men rigging horses in the barn. Without looking back into the room he said, "I'd like to borrow it, Mister Bjornson."

As Henry left the room his wife glared. "We have a rifle too, and a shotgun. Now that they're outside we could keep them out there."

Sam smiled at her. Very clearly Judd Pierce had done enough to earn the lifelong enmity of the homesteader's wife.

Sam said, "Let 'em go. Hopefully they won't waste any more time."

Bjornon returned with a long-barreled sixgun that had none of its original bluing on it. As he handed it to the marshal he said, "Bought it in New York and carried it across the plains."

Sam turned the big gun over in his hand. "Did you ever shoot it? Those loads look kind of green."

"Once, near the Missouri River. Some Indians rode too close. Maybe they was friendly, I never found out. I shot twice over their heads. They rode hard getting out of range."

8

A Fresh Headache

THE sun was climbing, there were birds in the trees along with a scattering of pigeons along the ridge of the barn. There were some things Sam had not noticed last night. One was a pen of hungry pigs making their grunts of annoyance at not being cared for. The other thing was a palisaded yard of chickens. He could not see them behind the slats of their fenced yard but he heard them. He also heard man-sounds from inside the barn, eased the door open more and raised the old hawgleg pistol for a rest on the jamb of the door. Whether Judd Pierce intended to keep his word about shooting Sam or not, the marshal's mind was made up about his own course of action.

Pierce had probably forgotten his death sentence; his overriding purpose at this juncture was to get away southward as quickly and as swiftly as possible.

When the first of them appeared outside the barn on the east side, Sam recognised the wizened man named Ezra. He had led his horse out and as he swung across it he called, and sat impatiently evening his reins until the next man emerged. This was the garrulous rider with the false good nature and slight accent. He glanced toward the house as the others crowded outside to mount their animals. The garrulous man said something to Judd Pierce, who looked in the direction of the house, said nothing but reined clear of the others, drew his sixgun as he approached the house and did not see Sam Brennan until he was almost to the corner of the overhang-shadowed rear porch, then Pierce made a guttural cry from deep down and started to raise and cock his weapon.

It was too late. Sam fired from his hand-rest. The old sixshooter bucked like a bay steer, smoke half blinded Sam, and the men shouted from over by the barn as Judd Pierce left his saddle in a flinging sprawl.

His horse ran, head out and tail up, terrified and blind. Behind him Sam shifted slightly and fired again. This time the men at the barn were flinging away in all directions. One man fired back, hit the roof of the porch and did not fire again, but another man did and this time the bullet seared a long gouge in the siding of the house.

Behind Sam someone fired with a big-bored rifle. Even the floor where Sam was standing reverberated. The smoke got thicker.

Sam turned, watched Henry Bjornson trying to flag the smoke away enough for another shot, and turned back. They were visible in different directions riding like the wind.

Bjornson was swearing when his wife appeared carrying a shotgun, a

139

formidable weapon but with a limited range.

Sam waited until hoofbeats were faint before going down off the porch and over where Judd Pierce was lying on his side with one arm outflung. His hat was lying ten feet away.

The Bjornsons joined him and stood silent and grim as the marshal sank to one knee. There was blood but Sam was reluctant to move Pierce, whose eyelids flickered and features twitched, but he did gently lift Pierce's coat where it bulged and retrieved the brown envelope, which he shoved inside his shirt.

Henry Bjornson knelt, ignored the marshal and very carefully eased Judd Pierce onto his back, an act which brought a sharp rebuke from his wife, but whose meaning became clear when Henry answered her roughly in English.

"A man like this deserves to die. If this makes him breather harder, good, then he will die sooner."

Sam saw the source of the bleeding

and for a moment rememberd his first sighting of Jess Hume. The same discolouration was beginning to appear, as was the swelling.

Sam watched Henry Bjornson open Pierce's clothing. Henry remained leaning for a moment before settling back on his heels. "He don't have the chance. How do I know? Marshal, in my own country I was physician. In this country I am a homesteader."

Sam stared at the large man. Why in hell anyone who could practice medicine would want to be a homesteader . . .

"I cannot be a physician in this country. You have to be licensed and in New York they refused to license me." Henry continued to sit back gazing at Judd Pierce. "You see; that old pistol did fire after all, didn't it? Look; you see that wound? If we rolled him over it would be twice as large in back where the bullet came out. Marshal, if you want to say anything, you can try, but I don't think he can hear you."

Sam gazed at Judd Pierce, he neither

pitied the man nor had anything to say to him, so he stood up, dusted his trousers and looked out and around. There was no sign of horsemen in any direction. He guessed they would come together again southward somewhere, and right at this moment he did not much care what they did.

He had those damned deeds in their brown envelope. Without Pierce they might as well scatter like leaves, and without those deeds that would be the wisest thing for them to do.

Pierce groaned, catching Sam's attention again. Henry had turned him on his side to look for the hole in back. As he held Pierce up he shook his head and gently eased him down. Behind Henry his wife surprised Sam when she said, "Isn't there something, Henry . . . ?"

Her husband did not look up when he replied. "Nothing. We could not even get whiskey down him. You see that swelling, well, it will turn blue quickly now. It is better that he stay unconscious. Get the marshal some coffee with whiskey in it."

★ ★ ★

As the large woman turned toward the house where her son was standing on the porch, quiet and motionless, Henry struggled to his feet and wiped his hands on a large blue bandana. "If your horse is still in the barn, marshal, you can go after them, but it would be a foolish thing to do. There are too many of them. Well; come along and get your coffee."

Sam said. "What about him?"

Henry shrugged. "By the time you drink your coffee he will be dead. We could move him, for what reason? A dying man might just as well die where he lies when there is no hope and he knows nothing. Come along."

Sam considered Judd Pierce one more time then moved to follow the large settler when Olaf suddenly called out.

"There! Riders coming from the south. I think there is four of them."

His father stopped, shaded his eyes for a moment then looked at Sam Brennan, "Coming back so soon? For the brown envelope?"

Sam had no idea who they were. It did not seem probable the renegade rangemen would return so soon, or for that matter, return at all. Without their leader they were adrift. Sam could not recall any of the others having the kind of ability Pierce'd had, the kind of stubborn motivation.

The Bjornsons were on their porch. Only Olaf did not have a gun. The riders halted well beyond gun range and seemed to be palavering out there while looking in the direction of the house.

Sam went to the shade at the lower side of the porch, rolled and lighted a smoke. The sun was climbing, there was heat and off in the northeast there was a build-up of clouds, but no one noticed that.

Sam saw one rider begin walking his horse toward the yard. Sam gave a little start. It was Jonas Harwell. He told the homesteaders who the approaching rider was and Henry leaned his big-bored old rifle aside but his wife made no move to put the shotgun aside.

Jonas halted out a ways and raised his right hand, palm forward. Sam called to him. "Come ahead. It's Sam Brennan."

The harness maker was no less surprised than his friend had been. As Jonas reached the edge of the yard, saw the people on the porch, the dead man near the northwest corner of the house, and saw Sam leaning in shade smoking, he said, "We heard gunfire."

Henry Bjornson pointed without saying a word. Jonas rode on up and stepped from the saddle trailing one rein. "Sam, we didn't find hide nor hair of them. Not even any good tracks."

"For a good reason. Jonas, they cut back because one of them, feller named Hume, stole the brown envelope and was runnin' for it when he got bucked off and hurt an' these folks took him in . . . And those other ones came back looking for him . . . That's Judd Pierce lying yonder."

"Where are the others?"

"Damned if I know. They left the yard here and got shot at an' went every which way."

Jonas looked at the people on the porch and nodded. The woman said, "There's another dead one in the house."

Jonas nodded without much interest as he turned and flagged with his hat for the other riders to come ahead. When he turned back scratching his head before lowering the hat, he said, "You got the deeds, Sam?"

"Yes."

"Can you think of a reason for us to stay out here?"

"No. Unless these folks need help burying the pair of dead ones. The one behind us is Judd Pierce, the head renegade."

"Get your horse an' let's head for town. I'm hungry enough to eat a rattler if someone would hold its head."

As Sam headed for the barn the settler's wife offered to feed Jonas and his companions. Jonas declined and waited until Marshal Brennan appeared astride, then got back atop his own horse and led the way to a juncture with the other haggard, stubbled and tired horsemen. Jonas did not say a word, he simply raised his arm to point in the direction of Forsythe and the other horsemen turned in behind him. One was Dan Rupert. He hadn't cleaned up before riding away with the harness makers. He had enough beard for it to show salt and pepper. He turned back to ride stirrup with the town marshal, and for a solid hour they talked as the sun moved a little, the heat heightened, and those clouds no one heeded off to the northeast were firming up enough to show soiled edges and underside. Rain was on the way.

By the time they had windmills

and rooftops in sight everyone had mentioned their particular adventures, and when the lawman explained what had happened to the leader of the renegade rangemen, they all accepted that as Pierce's just fate.

Ace Billings was one of the town-riders. He listened to everything that was said and when there was a lull he wanted to know who the hell was going to pay for his damaged stagecoach.

He might as well have been talking to a bunch of mutes. Not only did no one answer but none of them even looked his way.

When they reached town and split up, the harness maker lingered out back watching the marshal off-saddle and corral the horse he had used, and pitch timothy hay to all three horses, which they were pleased about because ordinarily they were fed twice a day, once about sunup, again about sundown, and this time when feed was tossed to them the sun had not reached its zenith.

Sam walked southward with Jonas leading his livery animal. They discussed several things having to do with what they had passed through the last couple of days right up until Jonas asked what Sam intended doing with the brown envelope, and when the marshal said he was going to find the Douglases and give the damned thing to them, Jonas was thoughtful until they turned in down yonder and he had handed the reins to the livery barn dayman, then he strolled back into the alley, this time heading up the way they had come before he said, "I don't believe they're in town, Sam."

This had not occured to the lawman. The last time he had seen the Douglases they seemed determined to stay in Forsythe until their dilemma was resolved. "How can you say that when you been out posse-riding the last couple of days, Jonas?"

"Well, Ace told me when he agreed to ride with the rest of us that he had to be back in town yestiddy, so he cut back night before last, did his business in town, got a fresh horse and re-joined us. He said the Douglases was on the southbound when he got back, and left town on it about the time he started back to find me'n the others."

Sam Brennan turned in out of the alley to his corral and leaned on the top stringer watching his horses eat. Jonas settled beside him with one booted foot hooked over the bottom stringer. Sam finally said, "That don't make any sense, Jonas. They knew we were goin' after those damned renegades and their brown envelope."

Jonas leaned, watched the horses and said nothing until Sam pushed off the corral as he said, "Maybe Ace was mistaken," then Jonas commented tartly. "Go ask him."

The stage company's head Indian was not at the corralyard. That pock-scarred Mexican hostler said Ace had been there, briefly and had gone over to the tonsorial parlour for a bath.

When Sam walked into the barber's

shop the barber and a shaggy-headed rangeman he was shearing looked up in surprise. Sam gave them no opportunity to start asking questions. He asked if the barber had seen Ace Billings and when he got a sidewards jerk of the man's head he marched straight on through, emerged on the weedy back lot and followed a worn trail to a wooden shack with a pump on the outside where bathers were required to pump the tub full from outside before going inside to bathe.

He knocked on the door. An annoyed growl came back. "I'll be out directly. Keep your shirt on."

"It's Sam Brennan, Ace. Jonas told me you saw the Douglases leave town night before last."

"That's right. On the southbound coach."

"You sure it was them?"

"Of course I'm sure. Sam, no man who ever set eyes on that woman would ever mistake her for someone else. It was them all right."

"You didn't talk to them?"

"No. Why should I have? I wanted to finish givin' orders for which coach went on which run an' a few other things before I headed back to help Jonas an' the other fellers."

"Ace, it don't make sense. They been bustin' their buttons ever since they came up here to find something those renegades stole from them, then, when they knew I was goin' after it, an' in fact got it, they left town."

Billings sounded tired when he replied. "Sam, everybody did as much as they could. I don't care if I never hear of the Douglases again as long as I live. Right now I just want to soak, head for the roominghouse and bed down until next Thursday. We did all we could do. You shot that main troublemaker, another of them died from gettin' jumped off his horse, an' right now if I figure this right, the other ones are headin' out of the country like a bunch of antelope . . . by the way, did Jonas say anythin' about sellin' me that new set of harness? I asked him five or six times while we was chasin' shadows all over hell out yonder, an' he never once gave me a straight answer. Sam? Sam you still out there?"

Brennan walked away during the bathing man's tirade. He went to the jailhouse, unlocked the door and nearly stumbled over a letter that had been shoved under the door.

Even before he opened it he picked up the un-nerving scent of that haunting perfume. He went to his desk, sat down, put his hat aside and opened the envelope. He read its contents twice, the second time very slowly, and was still sitting with the letter in his hand when the old gnome who had the land and abstract office walked in squinting because of his line of work a man rarely got outside unless he made an effort, and the old gnome had not deliberately sought sunlight in many years.

He nodded without speaking and sank down in a chair against the front wall. "Hot out," he murmured, considering the lawman's look of concentration as he gazed at a letter he was holding. When there was no immediate response the old man sniffed and added a little more to his remark about the weather.

"Back in '61 just when the war was commencin' we had a springtime like this, and it commenced to rain an' didn't let up for three weeks. Some folks died of the pneumonia but about as many drowned, some of 'em right here in town when the roadway washed out an' turned into a regular river."

Sam put the letter down, put his attention upon the old man and said, "You ever hear of forging deeds to land?"

The old man nodded without any hesitation. "Yep. Real often."

"Did you ever hear of folks forging deeds when they had reason to believe the real deeds was around an' they could get them?"

This time the old man's reply was slower coming. "Well, maybe, I'd have to think back. But I can tell you when the Homestead Law came into existence there was forged deeds flyin' around like autumn leaves. Why? Someone forge a deed?"

Sam handed the old man the letter and it was to his credit, old or not, that he inhaled deeply of the faint aroma of exotic perfume before he began reading.

9

The Unexpected

JONAS HARWELL wasn't the least surprised when Sam took Ambrosia Douglas's note up to the harness works. Jonas dried his hands, picked up the fragrant note and rolled his eyes before reading it.

When he handed it back to the marshal, he said, "Well; why didn't he think of that before chasin' those renegades all over the countryside? Did you show the letter to old Schrader at the abstract office?"

"Yes."

"What did he say?"

"Pretty close to what you just said. If the damned fool had sat down and figured things out before takin' after Pierce, he could have faked the deeds and had them recorded down in

New Mexico by now, and when the renegade rangemen came along later with the real deeds, they'd be in the same fix as the orphan calf suckin' the hind teat."

Jonas returned to his work table. "Folks get so darned worked up they don't think. Douglas could have settled this thing without ever leavin' home." Jonas studied the big hide in front of him, reached for a tin template and positioned it on the hide as he also said, "An' that leaves you with the authentic deeds." He looked up and smiled. "If Douglas gets his faked one recorded that leaves you with momentoes of a mess that didn't really have a damned thing to do with your bailiwick, except for the wrecked coach and the disappearance of Dan Rupert."

Sam watched his friend move the template to different places and asked why he didn't just outline the template and start cutting. Jonas put an almost pitying look upon Brennan. "Because if a man takes pride in what he's doing, he'll use only the back for skirts, fender and the like, and use the shoulder, neck and belly, which stretches to beat hell and has no strength, for the part that gets no strain."

Sam leaned and watched for a while then left the shop. Ace Billings was haranguing hell out of a yardman in the wide pole gateway of his corralyard. When he saw Sam he left the red-faced hostler standing there and hurried to overtake the lawman.

They met in front of the jailhouse and Ace ignored the customary niceties of the weather, the prospects for rain and maybe politics; he said, "That damned stage went lame south of town."

Sam was opening the jailhouse door when he scowled. "What stage?"

"The same darned stage them highwaymen stopped up at the second spit of tree on the Edmonton trace. That stage is jinxed. One of my hostlers come back a while ago from deliverin' light freight in a wagon, an' met a cowboy who said there was a crippled stage about ten miles from town. Busted wheel an' axle. The only stage that went south since day before yestiddy was that same blasted coach that them highbinders robbed and tried to wreck. This was its first run since I got it patched up. Sam, I don't have but maybe one or two bent axles a year, never a broken one, an' of course when you lose an axle it breaks the wheel nearest the place where the axle let go."

Brennan eyed the agitated corralyard man. "Well, send a wagon down with a couple of men to rig it enough to get it back to town."

"I already done that.

Sam scowled. "What can I do?"

Billings stared, muttered something and went flinging back up in the direction of his corralyard. Sam watched him go, shook his head and entered the jailhouse. Danged fool; get all worked up and go squawking around town. He had never actually had much admiration for Ace Billings.

He put the brown envelope in his little office safe, slammed the door and frowned at it. Fellers like Ambrosia Douglas's husband shot from the hip; if he'd used his damned head he'd have forged those deeds and never left New Mexico. He would have taken possession of the old ranch and been sitting there as the *patrón* when Pierce and his friends got back with or without the authentic deeds, leaving them no way to file a claim.

Later in the day, up at Oliver McCann's waterhole, he encountered something that had not occurred to him. A rough individual who headquartered in Forsythe but who, as a cattle buyer, ranged over hundreds of miles of countryside, wondered aloud if maybe Forsythe didn't need two lawmen, one to get involved in affairs that had nothing to do with his bailiwick, as Marshal Brennan had been doing, and another one to mind what he was elected to look after.

When this grumpy individual had departed Oliver came down the bar to say this had been the attitude of local folks since the marshal had got tangled up with those folks from New Mexico, and they resented it.

Sam's retort was curt. "It wasn't those folks an' you know it. It was what happened to Ace's stagecoach; robbed and wrecked."

Oliver shrugged and went back up to his bar to look after a pair of bearded freighters who had just walked in.

Life pretty well settled back into its normal routine for Sam Brennan, the men who had been involved with him in the affair of the stolen land titles, and even for the homesteaders who now had an addition to their rather extended farmyard — two graves freshly mounded without headboards — by the time Sam encountered Ace Billings again, this time at Jonas's shop where the harness maker had finally agreed to sell a new set of harness to the head Indian of the

Forsythe Stage Company. Billings was grumbling about a price of thirty-five dollars for a set of harness and as Jonas counted the money he had been given, he grumbled about selling good harness to someone who never took care of anything.

They both looked up and nodded when the town marshal walked in. Sam asked if Ace had got his lame coach back to town. Billings was shouldering the new harness when he replied.

"Yes, an' like I told you that coach is jinxed. When we blocked it up to get the wheel off and examine the busted axle, we found that one end of the axle had punched right up through the inside floorboards, so now I got to get the carpenter to fix that. An' them passengers . . . "

"What about them?" Sam asked, with a vague misgiving.

"Well, the driver said they parted while waitin' for my wagon to get down there. The man hired a local cowman to rent him a rig so's he could continue on down to New Messico."

"An' the lady?"

"She said for her husband not to waste any more time, she'd wait an' come along on the next southbound coach. Only she fretted as the day wore along and eventually when the repair wagon come along, she stewed until they had the coach able to travel, then she come back to town with my yardmen who'd fixed the coach."

"She's here in town?" Sam Brennan asked in surprise.

"Far as I know she got a place up at the roominghouse."

Sam lingered a moment then followed Billings up as far as the corralyard where Ace turned in and the marshal kept on walking until he reached the roominghouse.

She was not there nor, according to the proprietor, had she returned since she and her husband had checked out a couple of days earlier.

Sam went out to the dilapidated but shady porch and sat down gazing pensively down through town southward.

Why hadn't her darned husband taken her with him? It wasn't that she'd have to go all the way back down yonder on saddleback. Ace had said her husband had hired a rig. Even the smallest runabout had room for two people.

Eventually the marshal went back down to the jailhouse — and got another surprise, only this time the note which had been shoved under his door was on rough paper and had been crudely written, nor was it signed.

It said very simply that the men who were holding Ambrosia Douglas would kill her by nightfall unless Marshal Brennan met them with the brown envelope which they knew he had.

Sam rolled a smoke, re-read the note and swore at the far wall. How could he meet anyone when there were no directions as to how this was to be accomplished?

He'd never had a very high opinion of the intelligence of the renegade rangemen he had encountered, and this situation made his opinion drop even lower.

He was still sitting at his desk when the water-eyed old gaffer who clerked across the road at the general store brought over his mail, something he occasionally did but was not obliged to do. As he put the mail on the desk, he grinned in a nearly toothless way and said, "My boss said I'd better get this batch over to you . . . One of 'em smells really pretty."

The old man hovered but Sam made no move to pick up the envelope atop the other mail, so he eventually sighed and scuttled back the way he had come.

This time the note gave directions. It was written in a more legible and articulate manner. Sam recognised the fragrance.

He was to bring the brown envelope south of town to a place called Point of Rocks because the road had been built around it, leaving a jumble of big boulders in place. He was to be down there before midnight tonight; he was to come alone and unarmed. The men who had Ambrosia Douglas hostage would trade her to him unharmed for the brown envelope and its contents.

Sam snorted. He had never gone forth on his lawman's business without his weapons. No one but a plain idiot would expect a professional lawman to ride to such a meeting without a gun.

He was gazing at the fragrant note when Jonas walked in mopping off sweat with a big red bandana. Without a word Sam handed the harness maker the first note, then the second one.

Jonas went to a chair to read them. As always, he took his time. After the second reading he raised his head a little. "Now what the hell," he said plaintively. "I thought they was out of the country."

Sam related what he had learned from Ace Billings and the proprietor of the roominghouse. Jonas's eyes widened. "You mean they was here in town when they grabbed her?"

Sam shrugged. "Just about had to be."

"My guess, partner, is that they grabbed her when they saw her, but I'll bet a new hat they was hidin' in town to grab you. You're the one with their darned papers. She didn't have them. They'd have made sure of that, an' likely she told them you had them. Women are sly critters; if she could get them to come after you that would buy her husband enough time to get down to New Mexico."

Sam, who had not got that far along in his reasoning, let go with a loud sigh. "Real decent of her, Jonas."

"Well, she had to get time for her husband to get down yonder, an' she probably figured that by now you had those darned deeds, since the fellers who grabbed her obviously didn't have them, or they wouldn't have snatched her . . . You're not going alone, are you?"

Sam leaned on the desk. "Jonas, that

stretch of road between town an' Point of Rocks is flat, open country."

"Not in the dark it isn't, Sam."

They eyed each other over a long period of silence before the harness maker spoke again. "You go down the road like it says. Dark or not they'll be watching like hawks. While they're watchin' you I'll ride around them an' come in from the east."

"On foot, Jonas?"

"Naturally on foot, the last few hundred yards anyway. I'd like to bring Dan Rupert along too. He's got reason to want a crack at those sons of bitches."

Sam studied his hands while considering this. One man, especially one as *coyote* as the harness maker, might be able to bring it off. There was another consideration, without Judd Pierce and Jess Hume, there could still be at least four renegade rangemen, and intelligent or not, all any man with fair eyesight and a good trigger-finger had to do was function by instinct when he felt threatened.

Jonas shot up to his feet, dropped the notes atop the desk and had reached the door before Marshal Brennan said, "Better me in front for them to watch while you sneak up in back without a helper."

Jonas hesitated in the doorway, then shrugged and left the jailhouse. His last words were: "Shove the sixgun under your shirt in back. I'll have my sixgun and a shotgun."

Sam had not needed that bit about concealing his sixgun. What he was not pleased about was that remark about a shotgun. No question about it, if Jonas could get close enough his shotgun would be worth two or three Dan Ruperts, but while a shotgun could cut a barrel in two at close range, it was not a preferred weapon at any greater range.

Sam had dinner at the cafe, went up to the tonsorial parlour for the key to the bath-house and went out back to soak for a while. When he re-appeared on Main Street that unpleasant rough cattle buyer accosted him with a sour comment about lawmen who neglected their duties, and when Sam asked what, specifically, he had neglected the cranky man said his wife's cat had been up in the cottonwood tree behind their residence for two days and could not be coaxed down, and it was the duty of the town marshal to take care of things like that.

Sam stood considering the big, unpleasant man for a while, then hit him on the slant of the jaw with his body turning in behind the blow. For one second the cattle buyer's eyes bulged in surprise, then he went over backwards half on, half off, the plankwalk.

Across the road two women wearing bonnets and carrying string shopping bags, stopped stone still. One of them waited until Marshal Brennan stepped over the unconscious man to continue southward, then she addressed her companion in a spiteful tone. "Good.

Now maybe that lout will set a ladder up and get that cat down. I've had to listen to it caterwauling for two days."

The second woman was gazing at the sprawling man half in roadway dust when she said, "Wouldn't it have been easier just to go up there and help him get the cat down?"

"Humph! Come along, Nettie. You don't live next door to that oaf and his shrew of a wife."

Oliver came out to sweep off his length of plankwalk and stopped stone still, staring. From across the road Jonas called over to him. "Passed out from that whiskey you peddle."

An old man who had slipped into a nearby dog trot to pee, emerged into the roadway fumbling with buttons as he said, "No such thing, Jonas. Sam Brennan hit him. I seen it happen."

Jonas's reply to that was grumpy. "Well, good. I've wanted to do that for years."

Oliver helped the injured man to his

feet, leaned him against the wall, and held him there until the cattle buyer's eyes slowly focused. Oliver put an arm around his own shoulder and half led, half dragged the cattle buyer up to his spindle doors and beyond, to the bar where he leaned the dazed man and went behind the bar to fill a jolt glass and take it down where he handed it to the injured man.

The cattle buyer did as he'd been doing for thirty years, cocked his head back to drop the jolt straight down. But this time he groaned, worked his jaw sideways for a moment then did away with the jolt.

He blew out a ragged breath and shoved the glass forward to be re-filled. As Oliver was obliging the big, lumpy man settled against the bar on legs that were no longer rubbery, and said, "Now what'n hell did he do that for? All I done was ask him to help me get my wife's darn cat down out of a tree."

Oliver handed over the second jolt as

he said, "Didn't you know, Pelton?"

"Know what? Is this whiskey on the house?"

"Yes. Drink it down. Didn't you know Sam Brennan don't like cats?"

"How would I know that?"

"Now you do. Drink it down."

The cattle buyer felt much revived after the second jolt went down. He scowled ferociously. "If I'd known I'd have been set for him. Next time we meet — "

"Next time you meet, don't mention cats."

"I'll wring his damned neck!"

"Pelton, take my advice. Forget it. You jump Sam Brennan and he'll open you up like a gutted snowbird. You haven't been around town enough to see him in action. Just nod like nothing happened. If you don't, whiskey won't bring you around."

"Is this second jolt on the house too?"

"Yes."

"Oliver, you're a good friend."

"Remember what I said."

"What in hell fired him up just because I said my wife's darned cat was in a tree?"

"I told you. He don't like cats. Otherwise he might have somethin' else on his mind."

Oliver was not the only person in Forsythe who thought that way. In fact there was only one other person who knew the facts, and he was about as likely to offer an explanation to the marshal's sudden lashing out, as were those two fellers up yonder in the yard of the homesteaders.

He was Jonas Harwell.

10

A Sickle Moon

SAM considered the position of the lowering sun, decided he had plenty of time; ten miles was not much of a ride, and before going out back to saddle up, he put a belly-gun in his right boot and put a second one up his left sleeve where he secured it with a coarse rubber band.

Jonas appeared without his apron and wearing his hat, something he rarely did in town. He leaned on the corral watching as he said, "Dan Rupert went out on an eastbound stage."

Sam's response to that was about what Jonas could have expected since Sam had not been favourable to having Dan involved. "Don't need him anyway."

"There's goin' to be maybe four of 'em, Sam."

Brennan dropped the stirrup leather on the left side as he looked around. "Unless you rattle rocks like a greenhorn, you ought to be able to make it. I won't be down there until dusk."

Jonas spat, studied the stocky saddled horse and without another word walked back the way he had come.

He stopped out front of the jailhouse to watch a big old freight wagon pass down the centre of the roadway, forcing what little traffic there was to squeeze around on both sides. If Sam had seen that he'd have collared the freighter. In Forsythe, as in many other towns, there was an ordinance against big rigs using Main Street.

Jonas was in no hurry. He rarely was. He went over to the cafe for supper and missed seeing Marshal Brennan ride south of town at the lower end, and he too appeared to be in no hurry.

It was a pleasant late-day. In the northeast big cloud galleons were forming, huge and mostly white with soiled edges. There was no wind to drive them which meant they would not reach Forsythe until early tomorrow morning or later.

Range people would see this as a good omen, a promise of rain. In town folks had a different view; rain; especially heavy rain, made a millrace out of the roads and cut runnels in the land. It also made some folks house-bound.

Sam Brennan did not notice the clouds, they were behind him and he made a point of not looking back nor, for that matter on either side of the road. He knew they would be watching, perhaps not until he was down-country a ways, but he had no illusions of what the renegade rangemen would do. They probably knew this would be their last chance to get the brown envelope, which Sam had inside his shirt. If he had to, he would give it to them. In his opinion the authentic deeds would be worthless by the time they could get back down to New Mexico anyway.

He rolled and lit a smoke. Forging deeds, whether with the kind of extenuating circumstances that were involved here, was still forgery, and Sam was a lawman. But he had never been so much of a lawman that he adhered to the letter of the law. He believed more firmly in justice than he did in book-law. His law was common-sense law. Book law was either ridiculous or unenforceable more often than not.

In this particular case he would make the trade with the full knowledge that Ambrosia's husband was well on his way to doing what had to be done, which meant Sam would hand over the brown envelope with the full knowledge that the papers in it were going to be useless, authentic or not.

He anticipated no particular trouble, but in the event trouble arrived, Jonas would be out there somewhere.

Three miles south of town he encountered a cowman named Blake and was obliged to obey road-etiquette and stop to palaver. Blake was a bull-necked, greying man who ran cattle over many thousands of deed and free-graze acres. He was a good-natured individual and wondered aloud what the town marshal was doing so far south of Forsythe.

Sam had anticipated something like this and had a ready answer, "Just sort of ridin' out and around. This time of year there're strangers aboard. It don't hurt to keep an eye on them."

The cowman accepted this with interest. He'd been raided in the past by rustlers. Not lately, though, as he told Sam, but it was a good idea for folks to look around a little.

They parted, Blake heading toward Forsythe, Sam travelling in the opposite direction. He might not have noticed anything for a while yet, but his horse raised its head, pointed with its little ears toward a swale on the east side of the road.

There was nothing to see but

179

open country but the horse's interest heightened Sam's interest, particularly when the horse continued to be interested as they rode along. Ordinarily a horse's span of interest is very short unless there is reason for it to be otherwise. A loping coyote, for example, or bear-scent, cougar-scent, man-scent, where there was no reason for it, would keep a horse concerned until he was well past the place where his interest had been aroused, and this time Sam's animal retained his interest until they were a hundred or so yards on southward, then he lost interest.

But Sam didn't. He acted as though he did, and slouched along with the sun turning red as it sank lower beyond Forsythe.

Not until he came to one of the stone troughs established by freighters on the west side of the road near a stand of spindly pines, and veered off to water his animal, and while waiting for it to tank up, leaned across his saddle studying the easterly countryside. Even

180

then he did not see the rider until he was re-bitting the horse, ready to resume his way.

He was paralleling the road in the same direction the cowman had taken. Sam smiled to himself, reined back out to the centre of the road and continued southward. Once, he looked back. There was no sign of the horseman. If he'd been actually heading north toward town, he would have been in sight either on the road or the country on the east side of it.

He did not see the rider again until the road made a curve to pass around a bed of white granite and he looked back again.

The rider was coming southward but back a considerable distance, too far for the marshal to recognise him. He was not hurrying either. It was as though he was trailing Sam by that far back to make certain Sam did not have someone behind him.

Otherwise the road was empty. It was getting along toward the time of day when most travellers had sought, and probably found, a place to bed down for the night, either off the road somewhere or at one of the towns along the way.

Sam poked along. He had until midnight which was a long time ahead. With plenty of time to guess what was up ahead he settled on that renegade the others called Hank, the garrulous individual with the false smile and drawling voice who projected an impression of good-nature and an unhurried acceptance of things. He had impressed Sam, from the moment when he had stepped out of the trees to capture the lawman, as one of those people who made either successful horse traders or bankers; the kind of man whose shrewdness was hidden behind a projection of easy amiability. Cold blooded as a snake and a lot more clever in a devious, scheming way.

The other renegade rangemen Sam had met had impressed him as run-of-the-mill cowhands, good enough at their trade to get hired on, but individuals who, without ethics or honour, would be easily led by someone like Judd Pierce or the man called Hank.

He speculated about Jonas. Evidently the man trailing Sam had not been far enough easterly to see Jonas coming down-country, or maybe he had seen him from a distance and had assumed he was some ranch hand in the employ of the stockmen who ran cattle over this grassland territory south of Forsythe. Judd Pierce never would have made that mistake. Hank probably would not have either.

Beyond the curve in the road Sam stopped, dismounted, led his horse into a strand of flourishing underbrush and waited.

It was a long wait. Sam's warning that it was over was when his horse raised its head, grass protruding from both sides of its mouth as it looked steadily in the direction of the roadway.

Sam finally recognised the rider, it

was that older man, wizened and juiceless, the one his companions had called Ezra.

Sam allowed the rider to get several hundred feet past the thornpin thicket, then rode down out of there and for nearly half a mile Ezra was too occupied in trying to find Sam up ahead to glance over his shoulder. Sam smiled and raised his right hand. Ezra seemed incapable of moving for a long moment. He was too surprised at having been out-thought to return the wave.

Sam rode up beside him, dropped both hands to the saddlehorn and barely inclined his head as he said, "Evening. Figured you might like a little company. Awful lonesome down here."

Ezra reddened. "Thought you was up ahead," he mumbled, and relaxed. "Well; it don't matter does it?"

Sam laughed. "No."

"You got them papers with you?" The wizened man asked, eyeing the place where the lawman's shellbelt and weapon should have been.

"I got them. How's the woman?"

Ezra considered his answer before offering it. "She's all right."

"Who caught her in town?"

"It don't matter, does it?"

"Maybe not, only seems to me you might have wanted to grab me instead. I had the brown envelope."

Ezra raised his rein hand and started riding. Sam swung in beside him.

"We figured to grab you, but every time it seemed we could, someone came along . . . Like that big feller you knocked senseless. What'd he do?"

"Got obnoxious. How did you grab her?"

"It wasn't hard. She was goin' up to the hotel. We was in the alley. When she went past we grabbed her. If we couldn't get you Hank figured she'd do about as well."

Sam considered that reply; so Hank had indeed taken over from Judd Pierce.

Ezra seemed almost to have read the marshal's mind. "Judd did a damn fool stunt. But he was a feller who, once he took a dislike to someone, he went after them."

Sam's reply to that was dry. "You're right about one thing. Judd was a damn fool."

Ezra dug out a lint-encrusted plug of tobacco and worried off a chew. He offered the plug to the marshal and Sam declined. "Never was man enough. Tried it once and thought I was goin' to die, and sort of wished I would."

Ezra smiled, got his cud pouched into one cheek like a squirrel, expectorated and squinted down the road. "Another three, four miles," he said, almost amiably, spat again and looked over at his riding companion. "That lady told us her husband left her. He's a Texan. Hank said they do things like that an' he ought to know. He's a Texan." Ezra wagged his head. "Take a lot more'n just gettin' mad at her to make me pull out."

Sam said, "Pretty as a picture on one of them calendars the railroads put out."

"Yes, sir, Marshal. That's one thing we can agree about. Smells like flowers an' something' even nicer. An' pretty. Don't look at all like the old beaner who was her grandfather."

"You fellers rode for her grandfather?"

"Yes. I was there longest, nine years."

"You didn't figure you owed him anything?"

Ezra paused to jettison more amber liquid before replying. "He wasn't too bad to work for. Only after nine years with him, another six or eight years with other outfits here an' there, an' I had exactly what I started with. This old saddle, the same boots and spurs, the same bedroll. Judd was with him three years. He figured a lot, never stopped figuring. He figured out how we could own the ranch, sell it off along with the cattle and never have to fork a saddle again as long as we lived. Marshal, you can't turn your nose up at somethin' like that."

Again, Sam Brennan's response was dry. "Didn't do Judd much good, Ezra."

"Well; like I said, Judd was a damned fool."

Sam looked around. The roadway was empty as far as he could see, but visibility was becoming impaired with the final setting of the sun. "Tell me something," he said to the wizened, older man. "Just how do you figure to own the ranch an' sell it off?"

"Hell, by now you know the answer to that. We record the deeds in someone else's name. It was goin' to be Judd. Now I guess it will be Hank. Once the deed's recorded can't no one claim the place. That's New Messico law."

Sam considered the lined, weathered profile of his companion. Ezra might have been a good rangeman, but he clearly had not stopped to think about the departure of the Douglas woman's husband, otherwise he'd have guessed why Douglas went back to New Mexico, and again Ezra seemed to have read the lawman's mind, but in a way that made Sam ride for a while in silence.

"Even if Mister Douglas goes back down there it ain't goin' to do him no good. He don't have the deeds. We'll have them."

Sam's silence was prompted by his earlier idea that these renegade rangemen were not smart at all. He wondered if Judd Pierce would have wondered if the deeds could be forged.

Ezra surprised him with a question. "Was you really goin' to do away with him an' marry her?" Ezra saw the look on Sam's face. "That's what Judd figured. He said there wasn't no other reason for you to do all you did to help her. It wasn't none of your affair."

Sam did not know what to say so

he wisely kept silent, and that seemed to confirm in the mind of the wizened man that what Judd had said was the truth.

He jettisoned his cud and sighed. "Can't say as I blame you, Marshal. She's sure somethin' a man'd dream about twenty years down the road."

They had the Point of Rocks in sight. It was a massive jumble of greyish very old rocks, taller than a man on horseback, and stretched at least a hundred yards east. The only way the road builders could have kept the roadbed straight would have been to dynamite the largest rocks near the road, and that meant using wagons and teams to move the debris so the road could be held to a straight course, an idea that would have very little appeal to anyone, particularly since to go around the foremost boulders would not actually make much difference, the curve out and around was very gradual, not sharp enough to make a stage driver haul in his horses.

Sam squinted southeasterly in the direction of the backgrounding tumble of large rocks, which seemed to be smaller the farther east they went.

If Jonas was out there he would be invisible now that dusk was turning to night. If for some reason he was not out there . . . Sam shrugged. He could still make the trade, if that scheming son of a bitch with the false smile had not changed his mind about releasing the handsome woman.

He asked Ezra if the men at Point of Rocks had discussed keeping the beautiful woman and taking the brown envelope too.

Ezra shook his head. "She'd be worth it, except that we got a long way to go after we get the deeds, an' we got to travel fast. Too fast fer a female to keep up. Naw, you can have her." Ezra smiled broadly. "By the time she gets back down there, it won't make no difference."

They had little more to say until Ezra raised his arm. "There, atop that big rock. They didn't expect me to be ridin' with you. All I was supposed to do was make sure you come down this far."

The man atop the tall rock was leaning on a carbine peering intently in their direction. He probably could not make them out very well, but he certainly had heard them talking.

When they got closer he was no longer up there. Ezra said, "Marshal, if you snuck along a gun, take my advice an' throw it away before we get down there. There's bad feelin' about you shootin' Judd."

Sam nodded about the advice without taking his eyes off the field of huge boulders. There were no other such rocks anywhere on the road that he knew of, and if there had been he would have known. He'd been up and down this road dozens of times.

He cast one long, final look eastward before the big stones closed off his vision. He did not see anything, nor in fact had he expected to. It was just the action of a man whose life was shortly to be in more peril than it had ever been before. If there was an ally out there it would be nice to know it.

When they were abreast of the rocks Ezra said, "Hold it right here," and swung to the ground facing the boulders. He raised his voice slightly as he called into the thickening early night.

"All right. Come get him. He ain't wearin' his gun, but that don't mean much. I've seen 'em with hide-outs plenty of times."

11

The Killer

TWO men Sam recognised but did not know came out of the rocks, one with a carbine in the crook of his arm, evidently the same man who had been atop the biggest boulder.

They said nothing. One searched Marshal Brennan, found the boot-gun, grimaced and tossed it to his companion, went over Sam again, not as thoroughly this time, then stepped back.

Ezra led the way. There were narrow, twisted pathways through the rocks that debouched into a clearing where dozing horses stood, completely indifferent to their surroundings and the grinning, raffish man called Hank was sitting on a rock near Ambrosia Douglas.

Even in poor light she looked frightened as Marshal Brennan was herded into the clearing and told to stand still.

Hank was slowly masticating as he studied the marshal. He smiled, spat and said, "Well now, Mister Brennan, I said you was an obligin' feller; you'd be along . . . Ezra . . . ?"

The wizened man shook his head. "No one back there, Hank. No sign at all. He come alone."

Hank's smile was almost genuine as he returned his attention to the marshal. "I knew we could do business. You got the brown envelope?"

Before Sam could reply one of the men who had met him on the road sullenly said, "He had a derringer in his boot."

If that was supposed to annoy Hank, it did not appear to. He reproached the sullen man. "Well now, Ken, you'd have done the same thing. A man don't ride to this kind of a meetin' without takin' some kind of precaution, does he? Just the boot gun?"

"Yes."

Hank continued to smile at Marshal Brennan as he made a little gesture with his hand. "Here she is, Marshal. Scairt a little but good as new."

Sam looked at the lovely woman who looked straight back from large, dark eyes. It was impossible to tell much in nightgloom but she seemed frozen in place. Hank nudged her. "Say somethin' to the marshal. After all he come down here to save your bacon."

Ambrosia Douglas obeyed. "I'm glad you came, Mister Brennan."

Hank scoffed. "You could be nicer'n that. He took a risk comin' down here. Well, Marshal, answer a couple of questions for me an' you can take her back with you. We stole the horse in town for her to ride. You can return the horse too. Now then, you got any idea about them deeds in the brown envelope?"

Sam answered truthfully. "The feller who runs the land title office up in

Forsythe told me that if you can get these deeds recorded, the law in New Mexico'll make you owners of whatever the deeds include."

Hank nodded. "Dead right. Did it cross your mind to maybe ride down there and record them deeds in your name?"

"Nope. It never did."

"Well, it should have, Mister Marshal. There's one hell of a big cow outfit with all the stock on it waitin' to be claimed."

Sam regarded the seated man and gently shook his head. When he said nothing it seemed to annoy Ezra and the others. One of them said, "Damn fool. Never seen a lawman who wasn't."

Hank nodded agreement. "Sure seems like it, don't it? Marshal, where's the brown envelope?"

Sam pulled it out of his shirt and held it out. Hank took it, opened it, drew forth some old folded papers and held them to what little light there was

197

for a moment, then put them back in the envelope.

Ezra said, "All there?"

Hank nodded while regarding Sam Brennan. He made no move to arise nor tell the woman to arise. He glanced at his companions, who were watching him, barely inclined his head and said, "Marshal, I admire a man that keeps his word. Too bad we can't just ride off an' leave you with the lady."

That sullen man who had found the boot-gun hooked both thumbs in his shellbelt and seemed to almost smile. He stood like a man who knew what was coming and was ready for it.

Sam gazed at the seated renegade with the drawl to his voice. He recognised the cold look behind the false amiability. "You got the paper, Hank. I'm no threat to you. You can get back down to New Mexico — "

"You could telegraph, Marshal."

"How? Forsythe has no telegraph."

The sullen man was not the only onlooker who was becoming impatient.

His companion from the roadway said, "Hank, we're wastin' time."

That seemed to annoy the seated man beside Ambrosia Douglas, but he ignored the speaker as he looked steadily at Sam Brennan. Finally, he stood up, shoved the brown envelope inside his shirt, re-set his old hat and almost imperceptibly nodded to the sullen man as he said, "Marshal, there's too much at stake."

For the first time it occurred to Sam Brennan that Hank was not talking about one murder, he was talking about two murders; Ambrosia Douglas too.

He felt momentarily chilled. Killers were nothing new to him, but the rangemen he had run down after they became renegades, usually horse or cattle thieves, had not been murderers.

Hank was waiting for Sam to speak. When he said nothing, Ambrosia spoke in a quick, breathless tone of voice. "He kept his word. You have the deeds. There is no need for you to do this," she told Hank. "If you do, it won't just be stealing a ranch. You may get away with that. It will be murder. You will never get away with that. It will haunt you the rest of your life."

The sullen man laughed. It made an odd sound under the circumstances. But he knew Hank better than either the handsome woman or the lawman did.

Hank did not even look down at the woman. His gaze at Sam Brennan was no longer amiable. He watched Sam scratch his chest and his arm, waited for Sam to speak and when he did not say anything. Hank spoke quietly to the sullen rangeman. "Keep your horse close by. Give us ten minutes, then do it and ride after us." Hank's lips lifted slightly. "No better place. They won't be found until buzzards come circlin' an' by then we'd ought to be darned near to the border. All right?"

The sullen man nodded and half smiled. His companions went after the horses and left his animal hobbled undisturbed by the sudden activity.

Hank accepted his reins from Ezra, who would not look at either the lawman or the handsome woman. His expression seemed to imply that he had not known the hostages were to be killed. Maybe that decision had been made after he had been detailed to shag after the marshal. In any case he kept his back to Sam and the woman as he snugged up his cinch.

Hank looked at the woman. Sam thought he was having a moment of remorse, but if he was there was no outward indication of it. He turned his horse once then swung across its back, evened up his reins and without smiling nodded to Sam Brennan.

Ezra led the way out of the rocks to the roadway and turned south. Sam could hear them moving without haste. The sullen man said, "Sit down on the rock next to her, Marshal."

Sam obeyed and rubbed his forearm as he did so. The handsome woman was white as a sheet, something night-gloom hid. She addressed the man standing a few yards away with his thumbs hooked in his shellbelt.

She had heard the others address him as Ken; she used his name when she said, "Listen to me, Ken. I will give you five hundred dollars in gold if you leave us and go after the others."

Ken's contempt showed in his reply. "Lady, you don't have no five hundred in gold, but even if you did have, my share of the land and cattle will be a hell of a lot more'n that. It'll be somethin' like three, four thousand dollars."

Ambrosia had only one ace left and she played it although Sam, sitting beside her, thought what it must have cost her to say it. "Those deeds Hank has are no good."

That caught the sullen man's attention. He stared hard at her. "No good? They're are good as gold. Better'n gold . . . Why ain't they no good?"

"Because when my husband left he had made forged deeds. There is no way you can catch him before he has those forged deeds recorded."

Ken shifted his stance, dropped one hand unconsciously to the upthrust handle of his holstered Colt as he stared at the handsome woman. "You're lying," he said, enunciating clearly.

Sam Brennan took it up. "No she isn't. Her husband will be down there days before you'n Hank and the others can get down there. He'll have recorded the forged deeds."

"He can't get away with that, for chris'sake," the sullen man exclaimed.

Sam disagreed. "He can an' he will. Ken, your friends have rode all over hell for nothing. You've been out-foxed."

For five seconds the rangeman stared, then he stepped away until his back was to one of the big boulders. Sam held his breath. He had seen that look on men's faces before.

A quiet voice came out of the

darkness to the left and well behind the boulders where Sam and the woman were sitting. It was quiet but still carried well.

"Cowboy, you draw that gun an' I'll splatter your insides all over those rocks! Real easy now, lift out the gun with your fingers and drop it."

Into the ensuing silence came the distinct sound of a shotgun being cocked, first one barrel then the other barrel.

The sullen man did not move, did not even seem to be breathing. Jonas said nothing more, and the seated people watched and waited. Afterwards, Ambrosia Douglas was to say it was the longest period of her life. Sam could have agreed.

Ken gently raised his sixgun and let it clatter among the rocks. Jonas never hurried and did not hurry now. He wanted the killer to sweat. Eventually he came out of the rocks holding his cocked shotgun belt-buckle high. "Turn around," he said.

Ken's breathing was rough and audible. "No," he pleaded. "All I was goin' to do was what I was told. It wasn't my idea. I'd have let 'em go."

Jonas's voice did not rise even one notch when he spoke again. "You son of a bitch *turn around*!"

Ambrosia spoke quickly. "You can't do this, you'll be as bad as he is."

Jonas's reply was in the same quite voice. "Lady, I won't mind being that bad. He was going to kill you."

"If you shoot him I'll tell the law exactly what you did," she exclaimed, and this time Jonas laughed and even Sam Brennan smiled.

"Lady, you're sittin' beside the law," Jonas told her, then addressed the terrified rangeman. "Lie face down an' shove your arms in front as far as they'll go."

Ken obeyed and did not even raise his head as Jonas walked over and pushed the cold gun barrels against the back of his neck.

Ambrosia grabbed Sam's arm, certain Jonas was going to pull his triggers. Sam put an arm around her shoulders as he addressed the harness maker. "What took you so long?"

Jonas replied still bending over pressing the gunbarrels into flesh. "Took a nap. Well, you want to head for town or set out here an' admire the sunrise?"

Sam was in no hurry. The woman's perfume was working its magic on him now as it had at other times, but she disengaged herself from his arm and got a little unsteadily to her feet.

When Jonas stepped back and eased down the dogs of his scattergun he and the handsome woman exchanged a long look. Jonas smiled, Ambrosia did not return the smile.

Jonas booted the rangeman to his feet, went over him for weapons, found a big boot-knife which he tossed into the rocks and gave Ken a stab in the back with his shotgun, herding him over where the horses were standing.

Not a word was said until they were working their way out of the boulders to the roadbed, then Sam palmed the little gun from his sleeve and handed it to the handsome woman.

"Something for you to keep as a memento of this night."

She accepted the little gun, hefted it, looked at the marshal and raised her heavy, arched eyebrows. He nodded. "I would have if Jonas hadn't showed up. Better to maybe get shot than to sit there and be sure of it."

She pocketed the little gun and rode beside Sam for a long while watching Jonas and his prisoner up ahead. When the pre-dawn chill arrived and Sam gave her the jacket from behind his cantle she said, "Are you married, Marshal?"

He shook his head. "No ma'am. Never even came close."

"That's too bad."

"Is it? Why?"

"You would make a good husband."

Jonas, who had been listening, twisted

to look back. "Lady, he's got more bad habits than you could shake a stick at."

Ambrosia Douglas, a keen judge of humanity, had already made her assessment of the harness maker. "At least he would not have killed that man back in the rocks and you would have."

Jonas straightened around in his saddle and remained silent until the first weak streaks of dawnlight appeared in the east. It got colder too.

The prisoner rode with his head on his chest until they reached that stone trough where Sam had watered his horse on the southward ride. When Jonas told him to get down and tank up his animal, he said, "None of this was my idea. It was Judd who figured it out. All me'n the others did was go along."

Sam had a dry comment to make about that. "That's the same thing General Custer said, an' look where it got him."

Ken dropped down to drink, arose shaking off water and looked stonily at the handsome woman. "You made that up about your husband an' the forged deeds."

She shook her head at him. "I told you the truth, and now I'll tell you something else. None of you can get down south in time to prevent the forged deeds from being recorded. Not only that, but there will be someone down there waiting for you to show up with the genuine deeds. My husband told me he would see to that. They'll be waiting for Hank and the others."

Jonas considered the sullen man. "You're a damned fool," he said, in a conversational tone of voice. "Snug up that cinch and get on your horse, and if you want to make a run for it, this'll most likely be your last chance. Go right ahead."

Jonas was holding his shotgun in the crook of one arm. Sam smiled at Ambrosia Douglas. "Not *that* much of a damned fool," he said, as they watched the rangeman mount his animal and make no move to even back it away from the trough until the others were also mounted and Jonas gestured with his shotgun for Ken to ride up front with him.

The cold was as intense now as it would be. It would stay that way until sunrise, by which time Sam figured they would be back in town.

12

Clouds

FORSYTHE was stirring. The blacksmith had opened the pair of wide doors to his shop and up at the cafe the window was fogged solid.

As they were leaving their horses at the livery barn the proprietor walked in chewing a toothpick. He stopped dead still. "That sorrel horse the lady was ridin' was stole from old man Trench's shed, Marshal."

Sam was tired. "You can take it back up there," he said without even looking at the liveryman. "Feed an' grain these other animals. I'll be along directly to take mine up to the corral out back of the jailhouse."

The liveryman turned to watch the harness maker, the town marshal, and the handsome woman leave his runway. He wrinkled his nose. When his slow-witted dayman came along he told him what to do with the animals, and stood watching Ambrosia Douglas walking northward between the two men. She was something a man didn't see often; she reminded him of a wisteria bush that had grown at the corner of his parents' home back in Missouri. Sweetest fragrance this side of paradise and on top of that, pretty as a speckled bird.

She left them out front of the jailhouse. Sam and Jonas herded their prisoner inside where Sam pushed him toward a wall bench with orders to empty his pockets into his hat.

Jonas went to the hanging *olla* for a drink of cold water, turned back, sat in a chair and ran a hand across his stubbly jaw as he watched the prisoner.

Sam took the hat to his desk, sat down and leaned forward eyeing the prisoner. "What's your full name?" he asked.

"Ken Cornwall."

"Where you from?"

"Nebraska. Folks took up land there when they come from overseas."

"Where did you meet Judd Pierce?"

"When I signed on with that old beaner. Judd was his rangeboss. A good man, easy to work for, always friendly. You didn't have to shoot him, Marshal."

Sam leaned back and looked sardonically at Jonas. The harness maker was comfortably sprawled and content to just listen.

Ken reiterated what he'd said several times before. "That lady's lying. Her husband can't record no forged deeds."

Sam shrugged about that. "They tell me down in New Mexico whoever shows up with deeds and records them, gets whatever the deeds are to. In this case a big cow outfit."

"Judd would have figured about that," the prisoner sullenly said.

Sam was indifferent about that too. "Maybe. Only he's under the sod out

213

at that stump ranch." Sam eyed the prisoner for a moment. Then arose. Took down a copper ring with keys on it and as he faced around the prisoner gave him a fierce, hating look. "What are you lockin' me up for? I didn't do nothin' but ride along with Judd'n the others."

Sam stood holding the key ring eyeing his prisoner. In the eyes of the law that was almost correct, but there was still the matter of waylaying the Forsythe stage and abducting its driver. Maybe not good charges but the alternative was to let the renegade rangeman go, and he had no intention of doing that. "For suspicion," he told the prisoner and gestured for him to stand.

Jonas watched the marshal herd his prisoner down into the cell room, heard the lock being set in place and was still sitting sprawled when Sam returned to the office, barred the door to the cell room and returned to his chair.

Jonas said, "You hungry?"

Sam nodded. "Hungry, worn down to a nubbin, an' sort of disgusted."

They went over to the cafe, which was full of diners and loud talk until they entered. Then the noise abated as diners concentrated on their breakfast while occasionally casting furtive glances in the direction of the town marshal and the harness maker.

The cafeman took their order and brought their platters wearing a wooden expression. No one addressed them which was probably just as well.

One man, the town barber, stood up, paid for his meal and strolled in the direction of the roadway door as he said, "Fresh bar of soap out back an' clean towel, gents."

The door closed behind him.

The cafeman kept their cups full of hot java. Most of his diners departed and the few who lingered were as quiet as mice.

Oliver McCann walked in, freshly shaved and shiny cheeked. He sat down on the right side of Jonas, gave his order to the cafeman, then leaned around as he addressed Sam Brennan.

"Figured you might want to know. They got Mrs Pelton's cat down out of the tree."

Sam nodded without looking up.

"She climbed up there. Pelton don't like high places."

Sam nodded again, waited until the cafeman departed after re-filling his coffee cup and reached for it as Oliver also said, "Seen the pretty woman goin' in up at the hotel. Didn't see her husband. Somethin' happen to him?"

Jonas answered. "He went ahead down yonder. She's to follow."

That troubled the saloonman. "If I had a woman as pretty as that one I'd never leave her to look out for herself."

Neither of the men beside McCann had a comment to make. They finished eating, arose, paid for their meal and as they were turning toward the door Jonas reached over, patted the saloonman's shoulder and said, "You'll never have to worry about somethin' like that, Oliver. Not as ugly as you are."

The laughter trailed Sam and Jonas as they returned to the roadway. Sam said, "I'm goin' to sleep until day after tomorrow," and struck out for the roominghouse. Jonas returned to his shop, put on his apron and eyed the hide still spread atop the work table. He wasn't sleepy and now that he'd been fed he was no longer hungry either.

He had pretty well marked out the hide for cutting and was hanging the tin templates back on the wall when Ace Billings walked in.

"Well," the stager said, as he leaned on the counter. "As usual Sam wasn't around when folks needed him."

Jonas looked up. "When?"

"Last night. Some shaggy cowboys rode in lookin' for fun. It got a little out of hand."

"Over at Oliver's place?"

"Yeah."

Jonas faintly scowled. "I just sat next

to him at the cafe an' he never said a word about trouble."

Billings was unimpressed. He said, "After it was over folks wanted to know what they paid a lawman for if he wasn't goin' to be around — "

"What happened?"

"Some big old sod buster was havin' a beer. He said he'd rode to town lookin' for Sam. Them rangeriders got to hoorawing folks in the saloon. One of 'em spilt the sod buster's beer." Ace Billings paused as though recollecting something that had made quite an impression on him. Jonas growled, "Cat got your tongue?"

Billings stared at Jonas. "You're not goin' to believe this. That big old sod buster picked the cowboy up by the britches and the shirt and heaved him over the bar. He broke some bottles. Another cowboy came at the clod hopper and was doin' a fair job until he walked straight into a fist like a small ham. The third cowboy stepped back and called the homesteader. But he wasn't wearin' a gun an' that didn't set well with the other fellers in the saloon. Several of them drew their guns and waited. The cowboy put up his weapon, got his friends on their feet, but the one that got flung over the bar was so bad off the other two had to carry him. They left town with four or five fellers standing out front watching them."

Jonas leaned on his cutting table wondering why Oliver had not mentioned anything about that. Billings had one more thing to say before leaving the shop.

"Folks wanted to know who that clod hopper was. There was talk of maybe replacin' Sam with him. He told 'em he wouldn't have the job for ten times the money they'd pay him. Then he said he was a medical doctor by trade but had no license to practice in this country, went out, got on his horse and left town. Jonas, if he's really a medical doctor, we sure could use him in Forsythe. You got any idea how folks would go about gettin' him a license for doctoring?"

Jonas shook his head and went back around the work table. When he glanced up the stager was gone and it was beginning to drizzle. He went out front to scan the sky. Sure enough there was a build-up of rain clouds.

As he was turning to re-enter the shop someone softly said, "Mister Harwell?"

It was the beautiful woman from New Mexico. Evidently she did not require a lot of sleep either. She was shiny-faced and smiling. He stood aside for her to enter the shop first. Then followed her.

She looked around, looked longest at the hide marked and waiting to be cut as she said, "I wanted to thank you for saving my life."

He offered coffee which she declined. He went behind the counter where his apron would not be visible and told her it hadn't been as much his idea as it had been Marshal Brennan's idea for him to sneak in behind those men at Point of Rocks.

She nodded about that. "But I can't find him."

Jonas balanced the idea of telling her Sam was sleeping at his room in the hotel, decided not to and murmured something about her being able to find him around town, directly.

She placed a small under and over derringer atop the counter. "I want to return this to him. He gave it to me on the ride back to Forsythe. He had it up his sleeve. It was nice of him to offer it, but I really don't need it. I hope he'll understand." When she smiled Jonas inhaled deeply and exhaled.

"I'll be leaving on the evening southbound stage, Mister Harwell. I'd like to leave the little gun here in case I don't find the marshal. You could return it with my thanks."

Jonas nodded wordlessly, watched the handsome woman leave the shop and was still perched on the edge of his cutting table when Dan Rupert walked in coated with dust and with the smoke-tanned gauntlets of his trade folded neatly under and over his belt.

He paused to use his hat to beat off dust. Then went directly to the stove, filled a tin cup with coffee and had it almost to his mouth when his hand stopped moving, he wrinkled his nose and looked over where the harness maker was sitting. Until now Jonas had ignored the stage driver.

Rupert said, "You sure smell pretty, Jonas."

The harness maker sighed, stood up from the cutting table and eyed the whip. "You just come in off a run?" he asked, and got a nod as Rupert swallowed some coffee, which was tepid because Jonas had let the fire die down hours before.

"Yep, on the run over to Edmonton yestiddy an' just got back. Was that pretty woman here, or is that somethin' you started wearing?"

"She was in here. Left that belly-gun

to be returned to Sam Brennan. She's leavin' town on the southbound this evening."

Dan discreetly emptied the grounds from his cup into a nearby cuspidor and stepped over to lean on the counter, eyed the derringer but did not touch it as he asked why she had Brennan's gun. Jonas related what had happened down at Point of Rocks and the stage driver listened intently. When Jonas was finished he looked at the little gun again without making any move to touch it.

"That feller you brought back — is his name Ken?"

"Yeah. Why?"

"It was him, a dried up prune of a feller they called Ezra who favoured one of the others takin' me back into the mountains an' shootin' me in the back. I'd like to meet him out in the roadway."

Jonas went back to studying his layout. "You might get the chance. Depends on when the circuit-ridin' judge gets here, and what kind of sentence he doles out. Don't seem to me Sam's got much of a case against him; stoppin' your coach and takin' you off it."

Rupert considered those words for a moment. Then shook his head and walked out of the shop.

Over at Oliver's bar he heard about the brawl and the way folks grumbled afterwards about Sam Brennan not being in town when he was needed.

The whip, who was a friend of Marshal Brennan, had a comment to make about that. "What'n hell do they expect? He was riskin' his life to keep that pretty woman from gettin' killed, along with him. Oliver, was you one of the grumblers?"

"Well, Dan, for a damned fact he hasn't been around much lately. But there was somethin' else. That big clod hopper with the funny name is a medical doctor. Can you beat that?"

"Bjornson."

"Yeah. That's his name. A medical doctor who can't act as a doctor in this country because he don't have a license."

Dan Rupert forgot all about his friend being disparaged. He asked for a drink, got it, downed it and leaned across the bar to speak in a soft tone of voice. "You think he really is a doctor?"

Oliver nodded. After the way Bjornson had prevented serious damage, maybe even a shooting, in his saloon, he would have agreed that the clod hopper could walk on water.

"Got no reason to doubt him, Dan. Why, you know someone who needs a doctor?"

Rupert leaned farther over the bar and dropped his voice almost to a whisper. "Me. I need one. That's why I took the run over to Edmonton day afore yestiddy. They had one over there."

"They don't have now?"

"No. He packed up an' left for a bigger town couple days before I got over there."

Oliver leaned down. "You look healthy to me, Dan."

Rupert pushed the little glass away so he could lean still closer. "It's ridin' stages in all kinds of weather, settin' in cold water in winter and sweatin' like a mule in summer."

Oliver straightened back a little. "You got 'em, Dan? I heard lots of times freighters and stagers get 'em if they don't change jobs."

Dan also pulled back off the bar. "I'll go out there," he said.

Oliver had a misgiving. "All I know is what he told us after the brawl here. Don't take my word for it, Dan."

Rupert put a coin beside the little sticky glass and left the saloon. Oliver watched the spindle door swing to and fro for a moment. Then went up to his tub of greasy water to start washing and drying glasses.

It was later, late dusk, before his customers began straggling in. The cattle buyer whose wife's cat had got into the tree leaned on the counter looking at Oliver as he said, "Marshal's over in front of the corralyard talkin' to a real pretty lady on the southbound. Where in hell's he been all day. This time?"

Oliver stuffed the sour bag rag into his waistband and scowled. "You get that darned cat down?"

"Yes."

The local pool hall proprietor, a short man with only fringes of hair said, "His wife climbed the tree, he didn't."

The cattle buyer responded indignantly. "It's her darned cat, not mine."

Neither the pool hall proprietor nor Oliver McCann said anything. Neither did anyone else among the little tables or ranged up and down the bar.

The cattle buyer got red in the face, paid for his jolt and marched out of the saloon into a cool, wet but pleasant late evening. The southbound coach was still across the road, horses waiting patiently. The whip and a yardman wrestling with light freight which was to be tied in the boot.

Marshal Brennan was leaning on the off-side of the rig talking to the handsome woman. The cattle buyer made a sniffing sound and struck out for home, making no attempt to go anywhere near the stage.

The drizzle picked up again, only this time before long it turned into a genuine rain; not the flooding kind, nor particularly objectionable, yet anyway. The land drank deeply as the water fell.

There was no lightning nor thunder, just a steady rainfall. The kind most folks welcomed.

Jonas stepped out of his shop where he had been working by lamplight to deeply breathe of cleansed air, and saw Sam up yonder beside the southbound. He guessed who Sam was talking to, lingered briefly, until he was getting wet, then returned to the work table, where he took down another deep breath, only this time the fragrance was too faint, before going back to work.

He looked up as the coach went past, could see very little through his roadway window because it was streaked with water, and saw the town marshal turn into his doorway from out front.

Jonas said, "This ain't next Thursday," then he also told Sam about the homesteader cleaning out Oliver's place, and mentioned what Bjornson had said about being a doctor of medicine.

The latter part of Jonas's recitation Sam already knew. He picked up his little belly-gun off the counter and pocketed it as he said, "I wish she'd kept it."

Jonas asked why it should matter. Sam's explanation was simple enough. "Well, over the years when she come onto it, she'd think back to Forsythe."

Jonas looked steadily at his friend. "You mean, think back to the feller who gave it to her."

Brennan did not evade the issue. "Yes. I'd like to figure she'd remember me as well as I'll remember her."

"You'n me and just about every other feller who saw her."

"Jonas, you ever think much about re-marrying?"

"Well, every once in a while, but if a man couldn't have someone like her, he'd better off stay single . . . You?"

"Yes. I seen my share of 'em but never one that hit me like she did."

"You suppose that Douglas-feller appreciated what he got?"

Sam smiled faintly as he changed the subject. "Close up an' let's go over to Oliver's place. You work in that kind of light an' you'll end up blind as a bat."

Jonas took off his apron, dropped it atop the work table and followed his friend out into the brisk rain. Audible but not visible on the south trace was the sound of an old stage rattling its way southward.

13

A Murderer

OLIVER put it succinctly after the third straight day of rain. "I wouldn't want to be God. Right now folks in town are cussin' the downpour, an' just beyond town the cowmen are happy as clams about it. They don't want it to stop and folks here in town wanted it to stop yestiddy. Now you know, God's an awful long distance up there. I figure he can't determine where town limits end and cow country begins."

Sam Brennan added a little. "He couldn't please anybody no matter what, Oliver."

Down the bar Ace Billings had been listening. He turned a sour expression on the saloonman and the town marshal. "You want to see what He's doin' to my business, walk over to the corralyard. I got wagons and stages over there with adobe mud balls built up on the wheels dang near to the hubs. Four horses can't hardly move a vehicle if the driver stops it. The weight is too much for 'em."

Neither the marshal nor Oliver McCann had anything to say, but to Sam Brennan the stager's complaints simply confirmed his suspicion that God could never please everyone.

The downpour began to diminish in the late afternoon of the third day. People emerged to assess the damage.

There were runnels the length of Main Street, but according to oldtimers nowhere nearly as deep as the washouts caused by previous downpours.

The liveryman leaned in the doorway, paunch over his belt, chewing a straw. For a fact the air smelled cleaner and fresher, and with the passing of the cloud galleons the heavens were a beautiful pale blue from horizon to horizon.

The liveryman admired these things as he studied the roadway washouts. As had been said up at the saloon, God couldn't please everyone at the same time, but He had done a favour for the liveryman, who owned a strong, wide Fresno scraper, and a team of fourteen-hundred-pound horses to pull it.

About two days hence when the top six or seven inches of soggy roadway had dried out enough, he could hitch up, fill in the runnels, smooth the road down, and hand the town council a bill for the use of himself, his big horses and his Fresno-scraper. It should be worth fifteen dollars, but if they balked, why next time they could try and find someone else with the appropriate Fresno and big horses.

So, not everyone in Forsythe cursed the rain, but the liveryman was too shrewd to bless it either, at least not out loud.

Sam Brennan had an opportunity to catch up on the details that piled up in his jailhouse office. None of them were important, like reading the wanted dodgers that arrived every few days in the mail, and writing up the charges against his prisoner, whose sullenness had been increasing since the first night of rain.

His prisoner was not a talkative man, at least not in jail, although he may have been entirely different outside; most men Sam had locked up seemed to develop jailhouse-shyness, or reticence. It had never bothered Sam very much, it did not bother him now, but the fourth day, with sunshine, steam arising out front, and well-water tasting a little muddy, Brennan's prisoner rattled his cell for the marshal's attention. When he got it he looked balefully out into the little corridor where Sam was standing, and said, "How long? I got a right to post bail. It's the law."

Sam nodded; clearly this was far from the first time Ken Cornwall had been locked up. Sam said, "Your bail is a thousand dollars."

Cornwall looked shocked. Before he could begin ranting the marshal also said, "We don't have a justice of the peace in Forsythe, so the town marshal does about what he would do, and that includes settin' bail."

"A thousand dollars?" the prisoner exclaimed. "It wouldn't have been that much for Booth when he killed Lincoln."

Sam smiled. "We'll never know about that, will we? Your bail is one thousand greenbacks."

"When'll the damned judge get here?" Ken growled.

Sam had no idea. "Usually once a month, but that depends on what he runs into somewhere else. A murder trial, maybe, or rustling. Things that could keep him in some town for a week."

The prisoner retreated to his wall-bunk, sat upon the edge of it and glowered.

Sam returned to his office, listened to a commotion out front for a moment, then went to the window. The possum-bellied liveryman was dripping sweat in the direct sunlight as he worked his scraper up and down filling washouts and leveling the roadbed.

Jonas came down to the jailhouse looking pleased. As he dropped into a chair he said, "When folks get house-bound they get cranky. They want to lynch your prisoner."

Sam leaned back at his desk. "You like that idea?"

Jonas's smiled widened slightly. "No. They're not goin' to do it but it sort of amuses me. It shows they're comin' out of hibernation. By the way, when'll he be tried?"

"Hell I don't know, Jonas. When some circuit-rider gets here, an' don't ask me when that'll be."

Jonas shot up to his feet. "I need a somethin' cool to drink."

They went together up to Oliver's saloon and were surprised to find the place almost deserted. Oliver brought them both a glass of tepid beer and two small sticks of peppermint, which would make the beer taste cold.

Two days later with Main Street in good shape again, the circuit rider arrived in town. He was a tall, cadaverous man who looked like an undertaker in his black coat and britches. He even wore a black hat. His name was Alex Stewart and he'd been riding the legal circuit for nine years. He visited briefly with the marshal, explained what he would require in the way of documentation to try Sam's prisoner, then went up to the hotel to get a room.

Sam's assessment of Judge Stewart was that he came about as close to being a machine, and in fact a tired one at that, as a man could become.

Sam went to work on his documentation. The more he wrote and re-wrote, the weaker the case against his prisoner appeared to him to be.

The following morning he took the documentation with him to the cafe and handed it to His Honour, who ate like a horse and still looked like he was on the verge of emaciation. His Honour took the papers, nodded and went back to his meal, expressionless and silent.

Sam went out front, saw the homesteader named Bjornson over in front of the jailhouse and went over there. He did not mention the brawl at Oliver's place and neither did the homesteader. He sat down, declined coffee and leaned to place a bundle in a gingham cloth upon the law's desk. "Things we took off those fellers we buried out yonder." Bjornson watched Marshal Brennan unwrap the bundle, lift aside two sixguns and scowl as he unfolded a thick piece of paper.

Bjornson only spoke as Sam put the paper aside. "That was on the one named Pierce, the one who ran at you an' got shot off his horse with my pistol."

Sam nodded. "Two thousand reward in Wyoming?"

"Yes."

Sam considered the large man for a time before re-reading the wanted dodger. Why would a man carry anything as incriminating as that around with him? In Pierce's case Sam would never know.

Bjornson cleared his throat to get the marshal's attention. "My boy needs better schooling than he can get out here, Marshal."

Sam leaned back in his chair. He remembered Olaf very well. He also had an inkling about the homesteader's remark.

"You're talkin' about the reward, Mister Bjornson?"

The large man nodded.

Sam leaned forward, read the dodger again and looked at the personal items of Judd Pierce and Jess Hume. To collect rewards required more than just a letter saying the wanted man had been killed, it required physical proof. He pawed through the items, asked which items came from Judd Pierce and watched the homesteader sift them apart. He remembered which pocket produced each item.

Sam studied the effects. There was probably enough, along with his letter, but sometimes people who offered rewards a year or two earlier did not have much enthusiasm about paying them after a lapse of several years.

"I'll do what I can," he told the large man. "It'll take time."

"Olaf could get half the reward, then, Marshal?"

Sam smiled. "As far as I'm concerned he can have it all."

"But he didn't shoot that man."

"No, but I did, and I'll put in for the reward and if I get it, you can have it to send Olaf where he can get schooling. What does he want to study?"

"Medicine. Marshal, two thousand dollars is too much money to give away."

Sam studied the big older man. "When Olaf becomes a doctor he'll most likely save lives. What would I do with the money?"

"Buy some land, Marshal, and — "

Sam laughed. "No thanks. Rootin' in the soil never appealed to me."

The big man stood up. "I don't know what to say."

Sam also arose. "Don't say anything. If we get the money, then we can talk."

He went to the door with the homesteader, stepped out to watch Bjornson go around the tie-rack to untie his horse and climb into the wagon.

Bjornson raised his hand and smiled. Sam smiled back and was turning toward the office when the gunshot reverberated from the upper part of town somewhere. Sam felt only a moment of breathlessness, then fell.

Bjornson came down off his buggy seat with surprising speed. Up in the direction of the harness works Jonas appeared in his doorway. Across the road Oliver McCann pushed past his saloon doors wearing his apron.

Over in front of the general store a woman who had just emerged and saw the marshal go down, screamed.

Bjornson picked Sam up as though he was weightless, carried him back into the jailhouse and put him flat on the floor. He was working over the marshal when people came to the doorway. Without looking up the big man said, "A basin of hot water. Get some laudanum and clean cloth. Don't stand there gawking, *do it*!"

Jonas saw Sam being carried into the jailhouse as he yanked off his apron, ducked inside and re-appeared in a moment with his shellbelt and Colt buckled into place and carrying his sawed-off shotgun. He entered the corralyard where yardmen were milling like sheep. His appearance did nothing to reassure them. Several fled but the pock-marked Mexican hostler stood his ground as Jonas yelled at him.

"Where did that shot come from?"

The Mexican flapped his arms. He had no idea where it had come from except that the gun had been fired from the upper part of town.

Jonas crossed the roadway. People

saw him, some ducked into recessed doorways, others yelled that the shot had come from different locations. No one knew where it had come from. It had been a complete surprise. If there had been a second shot someone would have been able to place its origin, but one shot where none was expected was impossible to place, and because whoever had fired it had done so from hiding, Jonas could go from store to store, down dog-trots back again and find nothing.

By the time he had worked his way opposite the jailhouse there was a crowd out front. Inside, the big homesteader had organised the town black-smith, a greying man with a beartrap mouth and muscles where most men had none at all, and his helper to keep people out.

Bjornson's back bothered him from having to kneel over the marshal. He leaned back to wipe blood off his hands, saw the blacksmith watching, and said, "The weakest part of the skeleton is the back."

The forbidding-looking blacksmith smiled and nodded. No one knew more about aching backs than men who shod horses.

The blacksmith had a question: "Is he bad hurt?"

Bjornson leaned forward again as he replied. "Bad enough. If he hadn't been turning away when the shot was fired it would have killed him outright. As it is, you can see the bleeding. It's got to be stopped or he won't live another two hours."

"Anything I can do?"

Bjornson shook his head as he worked swiftly, large hands surprisingly gentle and quick. "Tore through his left side, broke two lower ribs. It's not a fatal wound unless he bleeds to death."

The blacksmith had a suggestion. "Once I seared the stump of a man who got his leg cut off. It stopped the bleeding."

Bjornson did not look up as he said, "Did he live?"

"No."

"I need more clean cloth and hot water."

The blacksmith turned to the people just beyond the door. He did not have to repeat the request, several men left in a hurry.

Jonas had no difficulty pushing through the crowd out front. A sawed off shotgun was the best way in the world to clear a path. Even the burly blacksmith stepped out of Jonas's way.

Bjornson was sweating rivulets. He raised his head to fling off water and saw Jonas. "Don't ask questions," he told the harness maker. "Go into the cell room and make up a clean bunk for him. We can't move him until the bleeding stops."

Jonas ignored the admonition about questions. He asked if Sam would live. For the first time the big man on his knees replied to that. He said, "He has a good chance. The bleeding is beginning to clot with the bandaging. Go fix a bed for him."

Two townsmen returned from the general store with a full bolt of clean cotton which the homesteader took from them with bloody hands.

When a large pitcher of hot water was brought, Bjornson emptied the basin and refilled it with fresh water, then rocked back on his heels to mop sweat off his forehead with a limp sleeve. He grimaced at the blacksmith, who smiled back. They understood about bending over for long periods of time.

Bjornson got most of the bleeding stopped. To Jonas and the blacksmith, the homesteader appeared as almost a miracle man. The wound was ugly and ragged, discoloration and swelling were beginning to show. Sam's eyes were closed, his breathing was rough and shallow.

Oliver McCann was out front. He turned and bellowed for the town to be searched, every house, every shed, every loft and chicken house.

With something to do other than

246

stand out there in shock, men peeled off. Oliver was wearing a sidearm, something he never did. Not every man had a sidearm but before beginning their manhunt they got them.

Bjornson finally rocked back, hands in the basin of pink water, watching Sam's face and breathing. He had done everything that could be done for the time being.

The blacksmith said he could carry Sam down to a bunk in the cell room. Bjornson shook his head. "Not yet. Maybe not at all. I want the bleeding to stop, not start again. Does anyone have a bottle of whiskey"?

The liveryman produced a pony from his rear pocket. Bjornson removed the cork and swallowed three times before handing the bottle back. The liveryman had expected him to pour liquor down Sam Brennan. Bjornson shook his head as he got painfully upright. "Later, maybe. Right now no stimulant."

Bjornson went to a wall bench and sat down. Again he and the blacksmith exchanged knowing looks. Out front a woman asked if they shouldn't go for the doctor over at Edmonton. Bjornson shook his head. "It's too far. Anyway, I heard he's no longer over there. The best you can do for him now is to leave him alone, just let him lie there. Shock wears off slowly from gunshots."

The woman leaned to stare at the big homesteader. "Where did you learn to stop bleeding like that?"

"From the Old World where I emigrated from. I was a physician over there."

The woman was impressed. "We need a doctor. What is your name?"

"Henry Bjornson. I can't be a doctor here. I am not licensed. I have a homestead in the foothills northeast of Forsythe."

The woman continued to stare for a few moments, then turned and pushed her way through the crowd.

Sam groaned. Bjornson was down on his knees again in a moment, but Sam did not make another sound.

14

The Bushwhacker

BJORNSON was hopeful but he kept it to himself. From experience he knew about how much blood a man could lose and still live. It was not a matter of measuring, but something that came with experience, and while Sam Brennan's clothes were bloody, and the floor around him and even the big homesteader was marked with blood, experience told Bjornson the danger was less than it appeared to be.

He stirred fire into the jailhouse stove, made coffee and by the time most of the onlookers had departed, he and the blacksmith shared mugs of black java, and the homesteader became more talkative.

To the blacksmith's questions about

the marshal's chances, he said, "A physician runs risks when he makes guesses about things like this. Be wrong, and you lose credibility. But I'll make a guess: Three weeks in bed and he'll be all right. The ribs will heal. He'll carry a bad scar to the grave."

To the blacksmith scars were part of living. He had his share of scars. In his line of work getting injured and scarred went with the trade.

He left to join in the manhunt, leaving the big homesteader sitting there gazing at the unconscious lawman and sipping black coffee.

His wife would wonder; he had only come to town to pick up a few things at the general store, and to talk to Sam about the reward. He grinned mirthlessly to himself. If the man on the floor died, there would be no reward, no higher education for his son. He had to keep him alive, if for no other reason than that.

He stoked the stove, knelt beside Sam and after inspecting the bandaging, leaned back, and met the steady gaze of his patient. Bjornson nodded, and Sam asked what time it was. Bjornson did not own a watch. "Maybe three, maybe four in the afternoon."

"How bad is it."

"If you hadn't been turning back toward the doorway it would have killed you. I think he was aiming for your chest. He hit you in the side, ploughed a furrow, broke two ribs and made you bleed a lot." Bjornson showed one of his rare smiles. "I'll keep you alive, otherwise Olaf won't be able to go to school."

Sam's eyes twinkled, otherwise his expression remained unchanged. Bjornson asked if there was pain. Sam nodded. "When I take a deep breath."

"Take only shallow ones."

"Yeah; that's what I'm doing. You patched me up?"

"Yes. I think you should lie where you are for a while before you are moved. It don't take much to start bleeding. I don't think you can afford to lose much more blood."

"There's a bottle of whiskey in the bottom drawer of my desk."

Bjornson shook his head. "Maybe tomorrow." He pushed up to his feet. "Try to lie still and don't take deep breaths. I have to find someone to stay with you. My wife will worry about me being gone so long."

Sam's eyes followed the big man to the door. "Mister Bjornson, I owe you."

Bjornson looked briefly at the marshal, nodded and left the jailhouse. Out front three old men were sitting like crows on a bench. They looked up at Bjornson. One of them said, "You leaving?"

Bjornson nodded.

The same old man jerked his head. "How about him?"

"Let him lie still. I'll be back in the morning. He needs someone to look after him until then."

One old man nodded, spat aside and said, "We'll do it, spell each other off."

Bjornson looked at them and waggled a finger. "No whiskey, and let him sleep."

They watched him cross the road. One old man said, "No whiskey? What kind of a thing was that to say?"

The man who had spoken first scowled. "He's a doctor. Done medical work where he emigrated from."

"Well, by golly, no whiskey when a man's been hurt bad. I never heard of such a thing."

Their discussion was cut short by several armed men coming around toward the roadway on the south side of the jailhouse. One of them was Oliver McCann. He eyed the three old gaffers as he said, "You see anyone down here?"

One old man looked annoyed. "Sure, that sod buster just left the jailhouse."

"I mean a stranger, most likely. Someone who might have been the feller who shot Sam Brennan."

The old men hadn't, they shook their heads and watched Oliver scuttle to the opposite side of the road. He was carrying a Winchester saddlegun and had a sixgun around his middle. One old man mildly snorted. "A saloonman with a gun? That's about as useless as teats on a man."

The town was deceptively quiet. There was almost no activity the full length of Main Street. Over at the general store every once in a while someone would enter carrying a gun. The proprietor was not in town but his clerk a grizzled, grey man named Hauser, helped the first three search the store, the storeroom out back and even the ice house across the alley, but by the time the fourth manhunter arrived Hauser, who had been on the frontier most of his life, told him there was no one hiding in the damned store and for him to get out and stay out.

The general store was not searched again.

Ace Billings returned solemnly to his corralyard after having joined others in the only genuine manhunt that had ever occurred in Forsythe, leaned his carbine inside the office door and went out back where two hostlers were readying the late-day coach. They were nervous, which they had a right to be. A killer was somewhere around.

One of the yardmen asked if the search was finished. Billings shook his head. "No, but mostly they've got a-horseback to search the countryside. He don't seem to be in town. Seems most likely he had a horse hid, and left town right after he shot the marshal."

"Is the marshal dead?" a man asked. All Billings could say was that the last he had heard, Sam was still alive.

An agitated tall man with a shock of tousled curly hair came into the yard carrying a rifle. He yelled at Ace Billings. "Avery from the gun works just come back to town. They got the son of a bitch cornered south of town at Point of Rocks. His horse give out on him an' he's holed up. Jonas is down there with some other fellers."

Ace Billings and his hostlers listened,

and as the tousled-headed man left the yard to carry his message elsewhere, Ace said, "Put the horses on the pole, see to it the coach leaves on time. I'm goin' down yonder."

As Billings hurried to retrieve his carbine one of the yardmen turned to the other. "What kind of a darned fool runs his horse down? Hell, all he had to do was head north into the mountains an' they'd never have found him."

The second yardman nodded. "Likely, but this feller maybe don't know the mountains. Or maybe he's got some reason for headin' south. Like makin' it over the line down into Old Messico."

The first yardman snorted. "Messico? He'd have to cross dang near all of New Mexico to get down there, an' runnin' his horse into the ground wouldn't be no way to do that."

Ace Billings did none of this kind of speculating as he saddled up and left town in a slow lope. People who saw him go and who had already heard that Jonas and others had the bushwhacker cornered at Point of Rocks, relaxed a little. The house-to-house manhunt was called off. Except for those three old tobacco-chewers down in front of the jailhouse, folks began to return to their normal way of life. It was the general opinion that whoever that bushwhacker was, Jonas would come trailing back into town later in the day, maybe about suppertime, with him belly down across a horse.

For the harness maker the situation was different. In the first place the forted-up bushwhacker had not ridden his horse down, he had accidentally lamed it when he was loping along and the horse threw his stifle.

It was one of those things that happens. Maybe the animal had a pre-disposition, maybe he had come down with a hind foot canting off a rock, but whatever caused it, the horse had considerable difficulty walking, let alone loping, so if the bushwhacker found any irony in being set afoot at Point of Rocks, the men who had been pursuing him, and had no idea the rider they saw with the lame horse actually was the bushwhcaker, when he turned the horse loose and forted up in the rocks, his pursuers became convinced he would only have done those things if he had seen them coming, and tried to hide from them because he was the man they were seeking.

As Jonas said to the possum-bellied liveryman riding beside him, it was possible the man with the lame horse thought Jonas and his companions were highwaymen and forted up to fight them, but it was more likely he forted up because he was the drygulcher.

When they had him backed into the boulder field and Jonas detailed a surround, then challenged the man they could not see to show himself, and he called back he would kill the first man to approach him, Jonas rested both hands atop the saddlehorn and spoke quietly to the liveryman. "His name is Hank, I'd recognise that drawl anywhere."

The liveryman asked who Hank was and Jonas told him.

While he was explaining the other riders, six of them, reined out and around the boulder field. Hank yelled at them. They did not answer but kept well out of sixgun range.

The bushwhacker fired. The sound was different, it was higher and sharper; he had a saddlegun. The surrounding riders rode back another hundred yards, dismounted and waited.

Out front, in the roadway, Jonas and the liveryman split up, the liveryman riding back northward the way he had come until he too was out of carbine range, and Jonas rode southward.

He called for the man to come out. He called him by name. When the answer came back it was curt.

"Come get me. I'll salivate every blessed one of you. Come ahead!"

Jonas dismounted, led his horse into some underbrush on the west side of the road, made him fast there and returned to the roadway. If his calculation was correct, the bushwhacker had returned to the same tiny clearing where he and his companions had held Sam Brennan and the handsome woman captive.

Between that spot and the south roadway the largest boulders cut off all view both going and coming. Jonas walked without haste to the nearest big rock. It towered above him.

The liveryman yelled, his voice was shrill and grating. "Hey, bushwhacker, we can set down an' starve you to death. Unless you can eat rocks. Leave the guns and walk out."

The answer came back profane and defiant. "Come get me. So help me I'll nail every damned one of you."

The liveryman tried again. "You darn fool — you know how many of us there is? Eight."

This time when the gunman yelled, Jonas was close enough on the far side of the huge boulders to place him; he wasn't in the little clearing, he was across from it in the direction of the road.

Jonas started inching around the south side of the huge rocks. He was careful where he stepped. When he could peek around behind the boulders he could glimpse that little clearing. If he went toward it, behind the foremost boulders, he was going to be seen.

He paused to dry his gun-palm on the seam of his britches, and to make a study of the area he had to cover to get close enough to find the bushwhacker.

There was no way he could get close enough.

The liveryman yelled again. "Hey, you darned fool. Another hour there'll be half the town down here. They'll lynch you sure as hell. Come out now an' we'll take you back alive."

"Sure you will," the gunman called back in his drawling, dry tone of voice. "Just like I didn't kill that son of a bitch, eh?"

This time when the liveryman called he sounded surprised. "You talkin' about Marshal Brennan? You didn't

261

kill him. He bled out a lot but he'll recover."

The bushwhacker was quiet for a long time. Jonas knelt and risked a peek. He saw nothing. He eased back, looked across where the rocks were smaller and was considering trying to get over there when the liveryman yelled again. "Hey, you only got one chance. Another hour they'll storm them rocks and kill you sure as I'm settin' here."

There was no reply.

Jonas got belly-down, put his hat aside and peeked out again. This time he had a glimpse of a leg as the forted-up drygulcher changed position, got into a place where he could not be seen from three directions. No question about it, he was going to make a fight out of it.

Jonas eased around, rested his sixgun atop a rock, aimed and fired. Dust and bits of stone exploded where the gunman was hiding.

Jonas cocked and took aim again,

but before he could squeeze the trigger the bushwhacker bawled and sprang out where he could see Jonas. He was raising his arm when Jonas fired again.

Hank was hurled back against the rocks. He forced himself upright and this time fired twice from the hip. Neither slug was close but they drove Jonas flat behind the rocks.

Time passed. Jonas kept his head down. The only sound was made by a horse lustily blowing its nose.

The liveryman yelled. There was no reply. He tried again, and got no answer that time either. Jonas eased up an inch at time until he could see the area where the bushwhacker had been. The man was in a sitting position, his back to a big rock, both legs out in front. He was holding a cocked sixgun in his lap.

Jonas watched him for a full minute. He recognised him by sight and was tempted to call out to draw his fire, but something about the way Hank was sitting, leaning slightly, made Jonas hesitate. The liveryman yelled again. The man Jonas was watching made no attempt to respond. He was beginning to list a little more.

Jonas rested his gun atop the rock, aimed carefully and hardly raised his voice as he said, "Hank, I can blow your head off."

Hank's head came up a little but his gun continued to lie inertly in his lap,.

Jonas spoke again. "You hear me, Hank? Toss the gun away."

This time the seated man answered. "Can't. Can't make my arm work."

Jonas called to the liveryman to approach the rocks from the roadway, and waited. Hank sat looking directly at the rocks which concealed most of the harness maker, and did not move even though he had to realise other men were coming in behind him.

Jonas took a chance and arose slowly. Hank still looked at him without moving. Jonas stepped over some rocks with his cocked sixgun aimed, walked to within a few feet of the bushwhacker and slowly lowered his sixgun. There was a dark smear of blood on the rock where Hank had been sliding sideways.

The bushwhacker said, "You son of a bitch."

Jonas leathered his weapon, went over, took the gun from Hank's limp hand and tossed it. He used both hands to straighten the leaning man. He looked for the wound. It was very small. Except for a tiny circlet of blood it would not have been visible at all.

The liveryman called. Jonas called back. "In here. He's shot."

"You got his gun?"

"Yes."

The noise of men grating over slivers of stone was audible as Jonas shoved back his hat and stared back at the man who was staring at him. "Hank; why?"

"Why? That son of a bitchin' town marshal made it possible for Douglas to get down, record his forged deed, and hire some fellers . . . I was the only one that got away. I come back to pay him for what he done. I know I hit him. I saw him go down."

"Yeah, you hit him, but he'll live."

"I'll still settle with him."

Jonas looked around as several men appeared. The liveryman leaned for a close look and said, "He don't look shot to me." Another townsman pointed. "You blind? That's blood on his shirt-front. He ain't goin' to bite you, get closer and look."

But the liveryman did not move. Those riders who had been a ways eastward rode into the little clearing. They had heard the shouting. They dismounted and stood as solemn as pall bearers as Jonas sank to one knee. "Hank, we got to wait for a wagon to move you . . . Hank . . . ?"

A townsman said, "He's dead, Jonas."

They waited a while before tying the dead man behind Jonas's saddle and starting back. The lame horse they left after pitching his bridle, blanket and saddle into the rocks. He could follow along at his own pace, or he could run free.

They did not get back to town until suppertime was past and half the town was dark. They left the dead man under an old canvas in a stall at the liverybarn and dispersed, most of them heading for Oliver McCann's establishment.

Jonas went up to the jailhouse where only one of the old men out front was still keeping vigil. They exchanged a nod and Jonas entered the jailhouse office where a lamp was lighted. He looked at Sam Brennan and said, "I brought his gun back in case you wanted somethin' to remember him by."

"Who was he?"

"You remember that smilin' unctuous one with the drawl to his voice?"

"Hank? He came all the way back here to — ?"

"Get some rest, Sam. You look

peaked. We got the next five years to talk. Anything I can do for you?"

"No. Unless you want to give me a bottle from the lower drawer in the desk."

Bjornson say it was all right?"

"No."

"Then you go to sleep without it. Pretty good doctor is he?"

"As good as I ever ran across, Jonas. We got to do something about gettin' him set up here in town."

Jonas nodded. He was tired to the bone. "We will. There's other things we can take care of after you're up and around. Good night, Sam."

"Good night, Jonas. Come back in the morning, I want to hear the details about Hank."

From the doorway the harness maker replied. "Yeah. See you tomorrow." As he closed the door and looked northward, he saw the light go out at Oliver's place. Some days nothing went right. He shuffled toward his shop.

TOP HAND
Wade Everett

The Broken T was big. But no ranch is big enough to let a man hide from himself.

GUN WOLVES OF LOBO BASIN
Lee Floren

The Feud was a blood debt. When Smoke Talbot found the outlaws who gunned down his folks he aimed to nail their hide to the barn door.

SHOTGUN SHARKEY
Marshall Grover

The westbound coach carrying the indomitable Larry and Stretch headed for a shooting showdown.

FIGHTING RAMROD
Charles N. Heckelmann

Most men would have cut their losses, but Frazer counted the bullets in his guns and said he'd soak the range in blood before he'd give up another inch of what was his.

LONE GUN
Eric Allen

Smoke Blackbird had been away too long. The Lequires had seized the Blackbird farm, forcing the Indians and settlers off, and no one seemed willing to fight! He had to fight alone.

THE THIRD RIDER
Barry Cord

Mel Rawlins wasn't going to let anything stand in his way. His father was murdered, his two brothers gone. Now Mel rode for vengeance.

ARIZONA DRIFTERS
W. C. Tuttle

When drifting Dutton and Lonnie Steelman decide to become partners they find that they have a common enemy in the formidable Thurston brothers.

TOMBSTONE
Matt Braun

Wells Fargo paid Luke Starbuck to outgun the silver-thieving stagecoach gang at Tombstone. Before long Luke can see the only thing bearing fruit in this eldorado will be the gallows tree.

HIGH BORDER RIDERS
Lee Floren

Buckshot McKee and Tortilla Joe cut the trail of a border tough who was running Mexican beef into Texas. They stopped the smuggler in his tracks.

BRETT RANDALL, GAMBLER
E. B. Mann

Larry Day had the choice of running away from the law or of assuming a dead man's place. No matter what he decided he was bound to end up dead.

THE GUNSHARP
William R. Cox

The Eggerleys weren't very smart. They trained their sights on Will Carney and Arizona's biggest blood bath began.

THE DEPUTY OF SAN RIANO
Lawrence A. Keating and
Al. P. Nelson

When a man fell dead from his horse, Ed Grant was spotted riding away from the scene. The deputy sheriff rode out after him and came up against everything from gunfire to dynamite.

FARGO: MASSACRE RIVER
John Benteen

The ambushers up ahead had now blocked the road. Fargo's convoy was a jumble, a perfect target for the insurgents' weapons!

SUNDANCE: DEATH IN THE LAVA
John Benteen

The Modoc's captured the wagon train and its cargo of gold. But now the halfbreed they called Sundance was going after it . . .

HARSH RECKONING
Phil Ketchum

Five years of keeping himself alive in a brutal prison had made Brand tough and careless about who he gunned down . . .

FARGO: PANAMA GOLD
John Benteen

With foreign money behind him, Buckner was going to destroy the Panama Canal before it could be completed. Fargo's job was to stop Buckner.

FARGO:
THE SHARPSHOOTERS
John Benteen

The Canfield clan, thirty strong were raising hell in Texas. Fargo was tough enough to hold his own against the whole clan.

PISTOL LAW
Paul Evan Lehman

Lance Jones came back to Mustang for just one thing — revenge! Revenge on the people who had him thrown in jail.

HELL RIDERS
Steve Mensing

Wade Walker's kid brother, Duane, was locked up in the Silver City jail facing a rope at dawn. Wade was a ruthless outlaw, but he was smart, and he had vowed to have his brother out of jail before morning!

DESERT OF THE DAMNED
Nelson Nye

The law was after him for the murder of a marshal — a murder he didn't commit. Breen was after him for revenge — and Breen wouldn't stop at anything . . . blackmail, a frameup . . . or murder.

DAY OF THE COMANCHEROS
Steven C. Lawrence

Their very name struck terror into men's hearts — the Comancheros, a savage army of cutthroats who swept across Texas, leaving behind a bloodstained trail of robbery and murder.

SUNDANCE: SILENT ENEMY
John Benteen

A lone crazed Cheyenne was on a personal war path. They needed to pit one man against one crazed Indian. That man was Sundance.

LASSITER
Jack Slade

Lassiter wasn't the kind of man to listen to reason. Cross him once and he'll hold a grudge for years to come — if he let you live that long.

LAST STAGE TO GOMORRAH
Barry Cord

Jeff Carter, tough ex-riverboat gambler, now had himself a horse ranch that kept him free from gunfights and card games. Until Sturvesant of Wells Fargo showed up.

McALLISTER
ON THE
COMANCHE CROSSING
Matt Chisholm

The Comanche, McAllister owes them a life — and the trail is soaked with the blood of the men who had tried to outrun them before.

QUICK-TRIGGER COUNTRY
Clem Colt

Turkey Red hooked up with Curly Bill Graham's outlaw crew. But wholesale murder was out of Turk's line, so when range war flared he bucked the whole border gang alone . . .

CAMPAIGNING
Jim Miller

Ambushed on the Santa Fe trail, Sean Callahan is saved by two Indian strangers. But there'll be more lead and arrows flying before the band join Kit Carson against the Comanches.

GUNSLINGER'S RANGE
Jackson Cole

Three escaped convicts are out for revenge. They won't rest until they put a bullet through the head of the dirty snake who locked them behind bars.

RUSTLER'S TRAIL
Lee Floren

Jim Carlin knew he would have to stand up and fight because he had staked his claim right in the middle of Big Ike Outland's best grass.

THE TRUTH ABOUT SNAKE RIDGE
Marshall Grover

The troubleshooters came to San Cristobal to help the needy. For Larry and Stretch the turmoil began with a brawl and then an ambush.

WOLF DOG RANGE
Lee Floren

Will Ardery would stop at nothing, unless something stopped him first — like a bullet from Pete Manly's gun.

DEVIL'S DINERO
Marshall Grover

Plagued by remorse, a rich old reprobate hired the Texas Troubleshooters to deliver a fortune in greenbacks to each of his victims.

GUNS OF FURY
Ernest Haycox

Dane Starr, alias Dan Smith, wanted to close the door on his past and hang up his guns, but people wouldn't let him.

DONOVAN
Elmer Kelton

Donovan was supposed to be dead. Uncle Joe Vickers had fired off both barrels of a shotgun into the vicious outlaw's face as he was escaping from jail. Now Uncle Joe had been shot — in just the same way.

CODE OF THE GUN
Gordon D. Shirreffs

MacLean came riding home, with saddle tramp written all over him, but sewn in his shirt-lining was an Arizona Ranger's star.

GAMBLER'S GUN LUCK
Brett Austen

Gamblers seldom live long. Parker was a hell of a gambler. It was his life — or his death . . .

ORPHAN'S PREFERRED
Jim Miller

Sean Callahan answers the call of the Pony Express and fights Indians and outlaws to get the mail through.

DAY OF THE BUZZARD
T. V. Olsen

All Val Penmark cared about was getting the men who killed his wife.

THE MANHUNTER
Gordon D. Shirreffs

Lee Kershaw knew that every Rurale in the territory was on the lookout for him. But the offer of $5,000 in gold to find five small pieces of leather was too good to turn down.

RIFLES ON THE RANGE
Lee Floren

Doc Mike and the farmer stood there alone between Smith and Watson. There was this moment of stillness, and then the roar would start. And somebody would die . . .

HARTIGAN
Marshall Grover

Hartigan had come to Cornerstone to die. He chose the time and the place, and Main Street became a battlefield.

SUNDANCE: OVERKILL
John Benteen

When a wealthy banker's daughter was kidnapped by the Cheyenne, he offered Sundance $10,000 to rescue the girl.